Vera

D0205464

Making
Waves

candy apple books . . .
just for you.
sweet. fresh. fun
take a bite!

Making Waves

by Randi Reisfeld & H. B. Gilmour

CANDY
APPLE

SCHOLASTIC INC.

New York   Toronto   London   Auckland   Sydney
Mexico City   New Delhi   Hong Kong   Buenos Aires

ISBN-13: 978-0-545-07529-9
ISBN-10: 0-545-07529-7

12 11 10 9 8 7 6 5 4 3 2 1   8 9 10 11 12 13/0

Printed in the U.S.A.   40
First printing, May 2008

To the great kids who were in 5th grade at the High Mountain Road School in Franklin Lakes, New Jersey, when I was writing this book. You are all so cool. You inspired me!

A special thank-you, love and kisses, to their teacher, Stefanie Greenberg.

—*R.R.*

Dedicated with love and gratitude to John and Harry; to Shannon Penney, editor extraordinaire; and Randi Reisfeld, who would definitely win American Idol if there were a category for fabulous, fun writing. And to Jessica and Aled, miracles separately and together.

—*H.B.G.*

Table of Contents

Chapter One

❋

Making a Splash

"Quit splashing!" Emily Taylor shrieked at her best friends, laughing and sputtering. Her dark curls were already soaked and plastered to her head. She had to squint against the reflection of sparkling sun on the pool.

"Then quit making fun of me!" One of Emily's two best friends, Jenna Lutz, giggled and sent another spray at Emily. Unlike Emily's hair, Jenna's bright red curls grew and frizzed when they got wet. Just now she reminded Emily of a Chia pet. Jenna's pale face and freckled shoulders gleamed with the tanning oil she'd slathered on.

"What's the big deal? She only said that you're

obsessing again," LJ Suarez, the third member of the friends-forever trio, called out. LJ's skin tone was naturally the beautiful golden color Jenna hoped to become. Her thick, black hair was pulled back into a ponytail. "And she's right!" LJ added with a laugh.

"What's wrong with wanting to look good when we start junior high?" Jenna demanded.

"You already have more clothes than a department store," LJ pointed out sternly. "Plus, September's still more than a month away." Trying hard not to smile, LJ — who Emily knew was soft-hearted, even though she pretended otherwise — sent a fresh cascade of water at her friends.

Jenna shook her frizzy head, plunged underwater, and swam off through the jungle of legs below the pool's surface.

It was already July, but the happiness of homework-free, lazy days spent at the Franklin Lakes Swim Club was still fresh and precious to Emily. For practically everyone she'd ever gone to school with, this was *the* place to be in the hazy, hot days of summer. Emily and her friends had been members since their kiddie pool days, but now they didn't need a parent with them. They rode their bikes to the club almost every day.

From the bike rack, carrying their beach totes (Jenna) and backpacks (Emily and LJ), they'd take the path through the rose gardens. The grassy walkway ended at a sign pointing to the POOL (left), SPORTS COMPOUND (right), SNACK SHACK, BEACH, AND BOATING (straight ahead).

Emily and her friends almost always opted for the pool area. Leaving the walkway, they would head past the sandbox and kiddie pool, where an army of nannies tried to keep their little ones from thwacking each other with plastic pails and shovels.

The big pool, in which the girls now splashed and goofed around, was surrounded by chaise lounges, stacks of thick tanning mats, and fluffy beach towels. A lifeguard tower was perched near the edge of the deep end . . . and that was where Tyler Cunningham, Emily's secret crush, sat.

Emily had known Tyler practically all her life, and yet she still couldn't help looking away whenever he turned toward her. This year, they'd been assigned to sing a duet together in chorus. Even if Emily was too shy to talk to Tyler, at least she'd sung with him.

He seemed to be watching her now, looking down at her from his tall lifeguard chair. Predictably, Emily turned her back on him just as Jenna whispered, "Guess who's checking you out?"

Fat chance, Emily told herself, hoping no one could hear how fast and loud her heart was beating. That happened anytime Tyler even glanced her way. She was plain, regular. She had blah hair and an average face with only her wide emerald eyes to distinguish her from the gazillion other almost-thirteen-year-olds in Franklin Lakes. Tyler, on the other hand, was tall and tan, a junior lifeguard with sun-bleached hair and crystal blue eyes.

But Emily wasn't looking into those eyes now. She was staring at the far side of the pool where the green bungalow stood, housing bathrooms, showers, and lockers for storing street clothes.

The immaculate bungalow was flanked by a dozen private little tent-shaped cabins — cabanas — with gaily striped awnings that faced the big pool. These were rented for the season by families who liked to relax in their own private shade and stow their dry clothes, summer reading, and after-tanning lotions. In other words, the superrich.

Not that anyone who could afford to live in Franklin Lakes was exactly poor. Emily knew that she and her friends were lucky to live there.

The town was a wealthy New Jersey suburb full of wide green lawns and dozens of big, fancy homes. Jenna and her family lived in one of those houses — which Jenna jokingly called her "McMansion."

Emily's family lived in one of the older homes in town. As far as Emily was concerned, the white house, with its country green shutters and hundred-year-old maple trees lining the front walk, was one of the very best.

Five blocks away, LJ and her family lived in a slightly smaller house, one with two front doors. Her grandmother and her uncle Ernesto lived in one side, and LJ, her mom, dad, and younger sisters lived in the other.

Emily, Jenna, and LJ had been best friends since third grade. That was when LJ and Jenna had rescued Emily from Sara Livingston's brat pack.

Speaking of which, Emily thought, as Sara and her dreaded posse strolled out of the Livingstons' cabana.

"Ugh, they're here," LJ said, tossing her head toward the three lanky blonds. With lots of attention-getting commotion, Sara and her side-kicks were settling themselves on lounge chairs near the lifeguard tower.

The same lifeguard tower, Emily noted with annoyance, occupied by Tyler Cunningham.

Jenna popped up through the water between Emily and LJ. "Ice Queen alert," she hissed.

"Give me news, not history," LJ grumbled.

The Ice Queens had gone to Franklin Lakes Elementary with Emily, LJ, and Jenna. Last year, they'd all transferred to the Bonham School, the most fashionable prep school in their fashionable town. They weren't missed.

Emily tore her attention away from the trio — and their nearness to Tyler. "And what do we do when we see the Ice Queens?" she asked, as if she were a cheerleader.

"Ignore them!" Jenna and LJ chorused.

"Oooh," Jenna added, laughing. "We're so cruel."

"Not cruel. Cool," LJ corrected her. "Anyway, if they're here, it's got to be lunchtime. Sara never makes an appearance before noon."

"I *am* kind of hungry," Emily decided.

"To the Snack Shack!" Jenna gestured for her buds to follow her. She waded toward the barn-like red building that separated the pool area from the groomed basketball, tennis, and volleyball courts.

6

Emily had always thought that the Snack Shack looked like anything but. On one side, the so-called shack boasted a poolside patio of umbrella-shaded tables, an indoor restaurant where most of the nannies and parents lunched, and one of two open-air serving counters. There, you could grab a burger, a hot dog, curly fries, a drink, a scrumptious brownie, or an ice-cream cone.

The second counter was at the rear of the building, facing the sports courts. Also on that side was the entrance to the fitness club — off-limits to Emily, LJ, Jenna, and everyone else under the age of sixteen.

"Hey, you know what?" LJ said softly, as they padded across the pool deck. "I'm not really hungry. I think I'm going to go down to the beach. I'll just catch you guys later."

Emily and Jenna looked at each other. Both of them knew exactly what was going on.

LJ had worked all winter to earn the money for her summer club membership. Her parents couldn't afford to pay for it, and she was too proud to even borrow the money that Emily and Jenna had offered. Babysitting, mowing lawns, and eating only at home, LJ had managed to save enough to join. Now LJ was working every chance she got to make spending money for the rest of the summer.

LJ had only taken a few steps toward the beach when Jenna called to her. "Hey, hold up!"

Emily added, "Yeah, wait. We're coming with you."

"You don't have to." LJ rolled her eyes at them. "I thought you were hungry?"

"We were," Jenna said. "But we looked at the Ice Queens and totally lost our appetites — right, Em?"

"Actually," Emily added, "I thought we could catch our lunch. Anyone for sushi?"

"Sushi, as in raw fish?" LJ stuck her finger in her mouth and pretended to gag. "Emily Taylor, you are so weird." She shook her head, and Emily could see her trying not to smile.

"She sure is," Jenna jumped in. "Why else would she be your friend?"

"*Our* friend," LJ pointed out. Grinning, she called, "Race you to the water!" and took off toward the steps that led down to the beach.

Following her friends, Emily hurried over the man-made dune planted with tall grasses, and scampered down the wooden stairs onto the warm sand. The club's white crescent of beach faced the smallest of Franklin Lakes' three lakes — the one that Emily thought looked more like a large pond. She, LJ, and Jenna had always called it Baby Lake. On the sandy shore of Baby Lake sat two paddleboats and a rack of canoes for members and guests.

Emily hadn't gone boating since the summer before, when the three of them, giggling and screaming as she and LJ tried to switch seats, had capsized one of the club's canoes. The water they fell into was only shoulder-deep, but the squishy mud underfoot made them yelp and shriek at an embarrassingly deafening pitch. And who came running to their totally unnecessary rescue? Tyler Cunningham.

Emily shivered at the memory of how, when he reached the beach, Tyler shook his head and laughed at the girls as if they were rowdy two-year-olds.

Not much has changed, Emily thought, a little while later. The three friends were still acting like toddlers. She had sand in her bathing suit and her hair, and her arms felt sunburned and grainy. She had to admit, though, there was something about being all sweaty, having your hair dry into gritty knots, and not caring how you looked.

"Is that the best sand castle *ever*?" Jenna squealed proudly.

"Wait, wait." LJ had run to the lake's edge and pulled out some drippy green goop. "We need a lawn," she said, hurrying back to the castle to plant the seaweed.

"Careful," Emily urged. "You'll knock over my trees." *Trees?* She'd lost it. The trees she wanted to protect were little branches of beach roses that last night's storm must have cut loose from their spiky bush. Risking thorns, she'd popped them on either side of the sand castle's entrance.

Jenna's stomach suddenly gurgled. "We should have built a sand restaurant instead."

Normally, Jenna would have blushed at the noises escaping from her stomach, Emily knew, but her friend's pale skin couldn't get any redder. "You're getting burned, Jen. Maybe we should move into the shade for a while," Emily suggested. "Grab an ice cream at the Shack or something?"

Jenna glanced at LJ.

"Oh, come on!" LJ stood up and put her hands on her hips. "I have a peanut butter and jelly sandwich in my backpack, and I can get an ice cream. Let's go."

10

They were all brushing sand off themselves at the bottom of the staircase, when Tyler appeared at the top. Emily had slipped out of her flip-flops and was holding on to LJ's shoulder for balance as she cleaned her foot.

Oh, no, she thought. She glanced over her shoulder at their abandoned sand castle and hoped Tyler wouldn't notice it. *What would he think?*

The answer came quickly. Tyler started to laugh. "Maybe you guys should build something like that for the talent show," he said, gesturing toward their masterpiece.

The annual Franklin Lakes Swim Club Talent Show was the high point of every summer. Open to kids from kindergarten through sixth grade, it took place on the last Saturday of the club's season. The show was always a smash, and always surprising — with wildly imaginative, talented kids competing all out for prizes.

There were awards given in every age group, but the best, Emily had always thought, were reserved for the oldest contestants. These were the kids who were competing for the last time, as she, Jenna, and LJ would be doing this year. Last summer, the club had given away an amazing theme park birthday party and impossible-to-get tickets to a Hannah Montana concert. Each winner also got free membership to the club for the following summer — which, Emily knew, would be a great prize for LJ.

"Build what?" Suddenly, Sara Livingston appeared next to Tyler.

The Ice Queens' frosty leader (the one Jenna had nicknamed "the Royal Icicle") was literally looking down her nose at them.

Sara's sudden appearance — and, face it, her nearness to Tyler — shook Emily so much that she took a step back . . . and tripped over her own flip-flops.

Emily fell backward into the sand. Her long legs flailed in the air, then tumbled over her head until she lay there, half on her back, half on her shoulders, wrong side up.

She could hear Sara's Cruella de Vil laugh. "I wouldn't try a gymnastics routine for the show, if I were you," Sara cackled.

LJ and Jenna tugged at Emily's arms to help her up, which just added to her humiliation. Emily didn't dare glance at Tyler. But that didn't keep her from hearing when Sara said, "Just think about it, Ty. If we do that duet for the talent show, we'll totally win."

Chapter Two

❋

The New Girl

The club was less crowded after lunch. Tyler was back from his break, sitting up in the lifeguard chair again, smearing more zinc sunblock on his nose. The Ice Queens were still there, baking on their mats, their stuff spread out on the recliners around them.

The sun felt warm on Emily's wet back. She sat at the edge of the pool, her legs dangling in the water. It was no longer churning with every splashing, laughing kid she'd ever gone to school with. There were only a few playing around in the water now — as if everyone else's grandmother had shown up and ordered them not to swim after eating. Emily sensed this, but she wasn't really paying attention to it.

Beside her, like a bee buzzing around her head, she could hear Jenna stressing. "It's not just my hair. I mean I could straighten it again — but then I'd wind up with these pukey split ends, and it only works for about a week anyway, and then I'd have to do it again, and again, and again. Oh, and did you hear that lipstick has lead in it? Not all lipsticks, but some of the best brands. So what do I do now? I mean I just started wearing the stuff. . . ."

"Can you find anything *less* important to stress about?" LJ scolded playfully, bobbing in the water in front of them.

"What do you think, Em?" Jenna asked.

"What?" Emily said distractedly, then added, "Have you ever seen that girl before?"

"Who? Where?" LJ and Jenna followed Emily's gaze across the pool to the Snack Shack.

There, slowly making her way through a gaggle of curious snackers, was a smiling brunette in loose-fitting cargo capris, a tank top, and flip-flops. Over her shoulder hung a canvas tote bag. There was something about her that turned heads. She certainly wasn't dressed to attract attention. And yet — she did.

Charisma. A word her parents sometimes used popped into Emily's head. She had never really understood what it meant until now. It was how people were drawn to you, fascinated by you, without really knowing why. It was one of those "either you've got it or you don't" kind of things.

The new girl definitely had it.

Jenna saw it, too. "How can anyone look so cool without even trying?"

They watched as the girl returned the smiles of the burger-flippers, plus the three boys who'd abruptly stopped playing Nerf basketball to stare up at her from the pool.

But her attitude was friendly, not flirty. She just seemed to be looking for a place to sit.

"I've never seen her before, but she seems seriously cool," Jenna said. "Too bad her instincts are way off."

Of all the groups to approach, the new girl was heading for the one least likely to be nice to her. It was a brave move, but a huge mistake.

"Uh-oh." LJ's water-wrinkled hands balled into fists. "She's wandering into the Ice Queens' turf. They'll eat her alive."

Greased and baking on their chaises, the three blonds were so tightly involved with one another that they didn't notice the new girl approaching. It was only when she tossed her tote bag onto an empty chair nearby that the Royal Icicle sensed an alien presence in their midst.

She lowered her huge CK sunglasses and peered over the top of them at the brunette, who wore no makeup and whose thick hair was bunched in a messy bun.

The new girl nodded pleasantly to Sara. In return, Sara gave her a cold once-over and turned her back on her immediately. At that, the rest of the Icicle's crew sniffed disapprovingly. Tossing their pale, bleached locks, they followed Sara's lead like blond lemmings.

The new girl's friendly smile wavered, but didn't totally disappear — although the Ice Queens' frosty rejection *did* make her flinch and pick up her tote bag.

"Ouch. That was harsh," Jenna said.

Emily felt her stomach clutch before she even realized what she was doing. She jumped up and dashed around the pool toward the new girl. Behind her, she heard Jenna sigh. "Did Em ever meet a puppy she didn't try to save?"

"Go, Rescue Girl," LJ murmured.

As Emily approached the new girl, she realized she had no idea what to say. *I saw the Ice Queens being nasty to you and I came to save you.* Yeah. That would sound cool. Right.

To Emily's surprise and relief, the dark-haired girl saved her the embarrassment. "Okay, not my best move," she piped up. "My first day, and I get rejected. I sure know how to pick them, huh?"

Emily laughed. "You could have done worse — but not much. If you're looking for a place to hang, come sit with us." She pointed out her group on the other side of the pool. "We've got plenty of room."

"Thanks. That's really cool," the girl said, looking relieved and grateful.

"I'm Emily, by the way. Emily Taylor."

"I'm Aubrey Foster. My family moved to Franklin Lakes last week. I just joined the swim club today."

"It's a great way to meet people before school starts," Emily said, as they walked toward Jenna and LJ. "Well, it usually is, anyway. . . ."

Aubrey's smile, Emily noted, could light up a room — or in this case, make a sunny day even brighter. "What grade are you going into?" Emily asked.

"Seventh," Aubrey said.

A group of boys passed by, poking and pushing one another to get the new girl's attention. The only one who seemed oblivious had sun-bleached hair, sparkling blue eyes, and zinc sunblock on his nose — Tyler, still perched in his lifeguard chair.

Just a peek at him and Emily's face went bright red. *Wait — Did he just wave at me?* Emily allowed herself to wonder for a second. Then she answered herself just as quickly: *No way.* Tyler was probably waving at Aubrey, but he was just too cool to look like a fool doing it.

Still, what if his smile and wave *had* been for her?

Emily shook her head, trying to clear it as she approached her friends.

"Hey, guys, this is Aubrey Foster," she said. "She's starting at Franklin Lakes Junior High with us in September."

LJ hauled herself out of the pool and extended her hand. "*Mucho gusto.*" She grinned. "I'm LJ Suarez."

"And I" — Jenna inserted herself between Emily and LJ, — "am Jenna," she said, tossing a towel to the dripping LJ.

"Lutz," LJ added with a sly smile.

"Thanks, LJ. It's true. Jenna Lutz. Unfortunate name." Jenna shrugged. "It could have been worse. My mom's maiden name is Fleckstein."

Aubrey laughed. "Hi, Jenna. And LJ. Nice to

meet you guys. And thanks again for bailing me out, Emily."

Jenna turned to Emily, wasting no time. "Did you see Tyler waving at you?" she murmured, as they cleared off a neaby lounge chair for Aubrey.

"Oh, he was probably waving at Aubrey," Emily said.

"No offense" — LJ nodded at the new girl — "but Tyler Cunningham did not even know Aubrey was there."

Emily rolled her eyes. *Not possible.*

"Um, I think they're right," Aubrey chimed in. "He did look like he was into you." Music sounded from a pocket of Aubrey's cargo pants. Emily's eyes widened as Aubrey pulled an iPhone out of one pocket, a Sidekick out of another, a beeper, and finally, a BlackBerry. She checked the screen, reading a text message.

"My mom," she explained, fingers flying as she texted back. "She's like a helicopter. Always hovering. She likes to be able to get me at all times. No biggie."

"She probably just wants to make sure you're okay," Emily guessed. "It's not easy walking into a place where you don't know anyone. It's kind of brave."

Aubrey sighed, still texting. "You get used to it."

There was something strange in Aubrey's tone. Emily picked up on it a second before LJ, direct as usual, said, "So what's your saga, Aubrey Foster?"

"Maybe she doesn't have a saga," Jenna countered.

LJ was on it instantly. "Everyone has a saga." Turning back to Aubrey, she went on. "You know, like where you're from, and how long you've been in Franklin Lakes, and why you came —"

"And who made those excellent cargos?" Jenna interjected.

"The army-navy store," Aubrey answered with a grin. "Both of my parents are in the military. I've lived on army bases pretty much my whole life."

"What's it like?" LJ asked, genuinely interested.

"You move around a lot," Aubrey said, sliding the BlackBerry back into her pocket. "This is probably the tenth place I've lived in twelve years."

While Aubrey settled back in her lounge chair, explaining how apartments in army family housing units were identical, Emily's mind wandered. *All that moving from place to place. Bet that's where she learned to make friends so quickly. She probably had to learn how to say good-bye just as quickly, too.* ·

As if Aubrey could read Emily's mind, she said,

"But now that I'm starting junior high, my parents have promised that this is our last move. I'm here to stay."

"Excellent!" Jenna cheered. "So we've got all the time in the world to find out about you."

Just then, Aubrey's BlackBerry sounded again. Glancing at it, she frowned. "Of course. Just when I meet some really cool people, I've got to go. Mom's made some random appointment for me. She'll be here in ten minutes. Oh, well." She looked sheepishly at Jenna. "Good thing there's not that much more to find out about me."

"Of course there is," Jenna insisted. "Like *American Idol* or *So You Think You Can Dance*? *T*Witches* or *High School Musical*?"

"And most important, Justin Timberlake or Joey Youngblood?" LJ challenged.

"LJ is all about Joey," Emily said, laughing. "And *American Idol*, for that matter."

"Joey," Aubrey agreed slowly. Emily thought she saw a weird expression on Aubrey's face, but then it was gone.

"Nailed it! I knew it, knew it, knew it," LJ exclaimed.

"The Summer Fest concert tour is coming to Madison Square Garden," Emily said. "Joey's the headliner. We're desperate for tickets, but

21

the good ones are already sold out and LJ's not sure —"

LJ cut her off. "Not so sure I want to go, anyway."

Aubrey's BlackBerry buzzed again. She glanced at the screen. "Mom's here, right outside the gate. I'm so sorry. Gotta go. But would it be okay if I hang with you guys tomorrow?"

"Absolutely," Emily said.

"Deal," Aubrey replied. "See you then!" Waving good-bye, she hurried to the gate and out of sight.

Chapter Three

❀

Life With Aubrey

As Jenna had said, the girls had the whole summer to get to know Aubrey. And Aubrey made it easy.

That whole first week, she showed up at the swim club wearing what seemed to be her summer uniform: flip-flops, cargos, and a faded tank top. Underneath was a cute but simple bathing suit. A canvas messenger bag ("So last year," Jenna had mentioned repeatedly) hung from one of her shoulders, and a faded beach towel was flung over the other.

"That girl," Jenna announced one afternoon, "could wrap herself in that old towel and still look awesome."

And she could swim, splash, and scarf down greasy Snack Shack hot dogs with the best of them, LJ had noted, clearly impressed.

Now, sipping lemonades, the best buds twirled on their stools at the Snack Shack's counter to wave to their new friend. She aimed a blindingly bright smile their way.

In just one week — during which her mom had beeped her to come home twice, once so that Aubrey could go with her to a dental appointment, the second time to help unpack boxes — it had become clear that Aubrey was turning the tight threesome into a fun foursome. "It's amazing how Aubrey fits in so well with us. It's like we've known her forever," Emily said, watching Aubrey walk toward them.

What Emily didn't share with her BFFs was that it felt like they'd won a prize, hit the lottery. Aubrey was cute and bubbly and outgoing. In spite of her harsh treatment by the Ice Queens that first day (and Emily was sure they were going to regret that), Aubrey was definitely going to be a hit in junior high.

Jenna, who sometimes had an uncanny way of echoing Emily's thoughts, suddenly piped up. "What's strange is that she could be really, really pretty, but it's almost like she's purposely trying not to show off —"

"Maybe that's why I like her," LJ said. "She's not all about looks. She really listens. She never interrupts to ask annoying questions — unlike some mop-topped redheads I know!" She winked at Jenna.

It was true. Aubrey had a way about her. She included everyone in the conversation and made them all feel like whatever they said was really interesting.

That Saturday, the day most of the parents and little kids overran the club, the girls went bike riding in the Franklin Lakes Wilderness Preserve. Only Emily had been there before. Emily's mom, who was easily as eco-obsessed as Leo DiCaprio, had taken her once. As they'd walked through the park, Emily's mom had sketched some of the critters and plants they'd come across, while Emily read about them in a wildlife guide.

But even though she'd lived in Franklin Lakes forever, Emily didn't know that the preserve had a bike path.

Aubrey, the newcomer, did! She was the one who suggested the ride.

The preserve was a shady oasis on the

searing-hot day, and everyone, even LJ, loved the place. "It's like *The Secret Garden*," she said, actually sounding awestruck.

"Yeah, but without a Snack Shack," Jenna noted.

"And no Ice Queens," Emily pointed out.

"Um, I thought of that," Aubrey said. "I brought some in my bag."

"You brought some *Ice Queens* in your messenger bag?" LJ teased.

Aubrey laughed. "Snacks," she explained. "I brought some snacks."

They found a picnic table in the shade of a huge oak tree. While Aubrey unpacked sandwiches, chips, and oranges from her humongous bag, LJ said, "So how's the hunt for tickets to the Summer Fest concert? I saw some on the Web — for one hundred and fifty dollars! Never going to happen."

"My dad might be able to get us some at work," Emily said. "His company gets tickets to lots of Madison Square Garden events — hockey, basketball, stuff like that."

"Well, I'm not holding my breath," LJ said. "What about you, Aubrey? Are you going to try to get some tickets to the show?"

"Um . . ." Aubrey hesitated. "I'm checking it out."

"Well, don't forget us if you score some," Jenna said.

"How could I?" Aubrey teased. "You're so unforgettable."

Jenna threw an orange peel at her.

It landed on Aubrey's shoulder. "Vot iz dis?" she said, pretending to examine the peel. "Orange bio-titus peel-oma!"

Emily laughed. "Of the family juice-est, drink-o-rama, no doubt," she said.

Aubrey looked delighted that Emily had jumped in. "An endangered species," she added.

Jenna, and even LJ, cracked up.

A few days later, Aubrey arrived at the club at about three o'clock. Emily was especially glad to see her, since Jenna was visiting her grand-mother for the afternoon, and LJ was working. The pool area was noisy and crowded, so Emily suggested to Aubrey that they go down to the beach.

The weather was perfect, not too hot or cool. Except for a few swimmers, Baby Lake was calm. Lazy waves lapped at the shore.

27

The girls had picked up straw mats to stretch out on. Emily was just about to slather herself with sunscreen when she noticed that something about Aubrey looked different. And it wasn't just that her pretty, thick hair was braided. Aubrey was wearing makeup! It was subtle — a touch of eyeliner, shadow, and mascara that brought out her gray-green eyes, raspberry lip gloss, and a hint of blush.

But when Emily complimented her, Aubrey looked almost embarrassed. "I forgot to take it off," she mumbled. "I was in the city this morning."

That didn't actually explain the makeup. *But whatever*, Emily thought as she lay back, flipped onto her belly, and let the warm afternoon sun soak into her skin.

She was almost asleep when Aubrey said, "You know that lifeguard, the one with the blond hair? I think he likes you."

Emily opened one eye and glanced at Aubrey, lying about a foot away. "And I think you've been out in the sun too long," she joked.

Aubrey sat up suddenly. She raised her sunglasses and looked at Emily. "You don't know, do you?" Aubrey said with wonder in her voice.

Emily rolled over and lifted herself onto her elbows. "What?" she asked.

"For starters, how cool you are. I mean, you've got a great sense of humor, and you're totally pretty, and —"

Emily squirmed, flustered. "Cut it out," she said. "I'm so average."

"See what I mean?" Aubrey shook her head. "Now tell me you don't see that what's-his-name —"

"Tyler?" Emily said quietly.

"Tyler," Aubrey repeated. "You don't see that he's interested in you?"

Emily laughed. "Where did you hear that? From Jenna, right?"

"Wrong," Aubrey said. "Everybody knows it but you."

Emily mulled — okay, obsessed — over Aubrey's observation for the next few days. LJ and Jenna obviously agreed with Aubrey. All three of her friends suggested that Emily go up to Tyler and start a conversation.

But no way! That was *not* Emily's style. What if her friends were wrong, and Tyler made fun of her? Some girls could let humiliation roll right off their backs. Emily was not one of them. If Tyler wasn't going to say anything, Emily wasn't going to say anything to him, either.

Until Tyler broke the deadlock. One day, out of the blue, Emily and her friends were chowing down at the Snack Shack counter when Tyler marched over. Looking directly at Emily, he said, "So what are you guys going to do this year for the talent show? You're going to enter, right?"

"Yeah. We're going to build a sand castle," LJ joked.

"And then I'm going to fall over onto it." *Did I think that or say it?* Emily wondered, blinking. Aubrey's infectious laughter confirmed that, yes, she had said it aloud.

Emily was sure she'd turned fire-engine red. She lowered her head automatically.

Aubrey, sitting on the stool next to her, elbowed her.

Jenna, on the other side, kicked her.

Emily looked up. At Tyler.

He smiled at her, then turned to Aubrey. "In case you don't know, the talent show is kind of a tradition at the swim club. Everyone up to seventh grade is eligible to participate — no talent required!"

They all laughed.

Tyler cleared his throat. "Well, let me know what you decide to do. If you're doing the sand castle thing, I'm not going to bother entering. How could I compete with that?" He grinned at Emily and walked away. She could have sworn that he winked.

Emily turned back to her friends. "They change the prize every year," Jenna was telling Aubrey.

"Except for the membership," LJ added. "They give away one free membership to the club each year."

"Hey, you never know," Emily said. "Maybe we'll win this year."

"Yeah, maybe this year the Ice Queens won't enter," LJ said sarcastically.

Sara and her crew had won the talent show three years in a row. They'd outspent everyone else on costumes, music, singing lessons, and dance routines. Everyone knew it. The Queens made no secret of how much it cost to put their winning acts together. It was more, Emily knew, than the price of a dozen memberships to the club.

And then Emily remembered. Not only would the Ice Queens enter the competition — but Sara was planning to sing a duet with Tyler!

Chapter Four

❀

Party Planners

In keeping with Emily's mood, the next day was cloudy. It was supposed to rain. Jenna decided it was the perfect time to introduce Aubrey to the mall.

They checked out H & M, Banana Republic, and Old Navy. Jenna carried a big shopping bag as she trailed Emily and Aubrey into Macy's.

Aubrey made a beeline for the cosmetics counters, but Emily hung back when a pair of gold earrings caught her eye. "Think LJ would like these for her birthday?" she asked Jenna.

"Not as much as she'd like to go to that Joey

Youngblood concert," Jenna quipped. "But yeah, those are cute."

LJ was babysitting the crazy Lasky twins that afternoon. The toddlers were totally into their terrible twos. They were also LJ's best-paying job.

The twins had driven away three other baby-sitters, so their mom was desperate enough to double LJ's usual rate to keep her. And LJ had something those other babysitters didn't. She could throw the boys a look that turned older kids into quivering wrecks, and left the little wild guys wide-eyed.

LJ's absence made it easier for Emily and Jenna to talk about their best friend's upcoming thir-teenth birthday — and the surprise party they were throwing for her at Jenna's house. So far, they'd had to do all their planning on the phone or through texts. It wasn't a subject they'd brought up in front of Aubrey yet.

Emily glanced over her shoulder. "You're going to invite Aubrey, right?" she said softly to Jenna.

"I've been stressing about that," Jenna admit-ted. "My mom said absolutely no more than twenty kids, and I already made up the list weeks ago. Aubrey would make it twenty-one."

Emily raised her eyebrows. "But I don't see how you could leave her out."

Jenna struggled. "I wouldn't. It just means someone else is off the list."

"Try begging your mom," Emily suggested. "She'll let you add one more person. I'll help convince her, if you want."

The girls fell silent as Aubrey walked over. "What do you think about this gloss?" She showed them a sample-sized lipstick tube decorated with pink, green, and blue squiggles. "This is just a tester. The whole line is coming out in September."

"Cute package," Emily said. "What color is the gloss?"

"It's a pale pink. They call it Rosebud." Aubrey held the tube out to Emily, but Jenna intercepted it.

"What brand?" Jenna wanted to know.

"'Cool Aid,'" Aubrey said. "It's new. They're marketing it to high school kids."

Jenna opened the gloss and peered at it. "When did you become a makeup maven?" she asked Aubrey curiously.

Aubrey blinked, confused.

"Maven," Emily repeated. "It means 'expert' in Jenna speak."

"What?" Aubrey blushed. "Oh, I'm not. I just heard about this brand. It sounded fun. That's all."

"Maybe there was an ad in *Elle Girl* or *Teen Vogue* that you missed?" Emily teased Jenna.

"I think maybe *Seventeen*," Aubrey said quickly.

"Oh, I don't get *Seventeen*," Jenna mused. "Maybe I should."

Just then, Aubrey's beeper went off. She glanced down to check it.

Emily thought she saw Aubrey's expression brighten. A second later, she wondered if she'd imagined it. "Whoops, I forgot," Aubrey said, looking serious again. "I promised my mom I'd, um, go with her."

"Go with her where?" Jenna asked.

"Well . . . she's got this appointment —"

"Dentist again?" Jenna guessed.

"Doctor," Aubrey said quickly, then glanced at her watch. It was an ancient Swatch, which had once made Jenna remark that Aubrey was the least fashion-conscious person she'd ever met.

"Is she okay?" Emily asked.

"Who? Oh, my mom? Um, yeah. I've just gotta go," Aubrey said. Waving good-bye, she hurried out of the store.

An hour later, after some more browsing, Emily and Jenna hit the food court. Between bites of sandwiches and gulps of bottled water, they went back to discussing LJ's surprise birthday bash.

"Why not call your mom now and ask if you can invite one more person?" Emily suggested.

"Okay, but what if she gives me a hard time, and I convince her, and then Aubrey doesn't show up? Or what if she gets a call from her mom and has to bail early — which, hello, isn't even a stretch?" Jenna argued. "I'm trying to pick my mom-conflicts carefully, Em."

Emily nodded. "Who else is on the top secret invite list, anyway?" she asked.

Jenna fished a piece of paper out of her bag and handed it over.

Emily almost spit out her water when she read down the list. "Sara Livingston?! You've got to be kidding." Emily waved Jenna's guest list at her friend's freckled face. "LJ can't stand her — and the feeling is mutual. You haven't sent out the Evites yet, have you?"

"No, I was going to do it tomorrow," Jenna said, looking sour.

"Well, if you haven't done it yet, it's not like Sara would even know that she'd been booted off the list."

Jenna crossed her arms stubbornly. "People can change."

Emily tilted her head and squinted at Jenna. "You're kidding, right? After the way she cold-shouldered Aubrey? Sara hasn't changed one bit, Jen. Unless you have a better reason for inviting her, I say delete, and spare yourself a call to your mom."

"Look, Emily, I know that whenever you see someone getting cut down or left out, you react," Jenna said defensively. "It's a total sore spot with you, and has been since third grade. And anyway, if Sara wasn't with her crew, maybe she wouldn't be so harsh."

Emily rolled her eyes and let Jenna's words hang in the air between them. In the end, as Emily knew she would, Jenna recognized the desperation in her argument. She shrugged, smiled, and sighed, "Okay. Maybe you're right."

Later that afternoon, Emily was sitting on the white four-poster bed in her room. She nibbled the end of a sparkly pink pen. The diary Jenna had given her last winter sat open on her lap. Too many of the pages were filled with daydreams and doodles about Tyler.

Today, she'd begun to write about the talent

show at the swim club. She could picture them, just her and Tyler (with Sara Livingston nowhere in sight), singing a winning duet.

Yeah, she told herself, *that's why they call it a fantasy.* In real life? Not a chance. Being forced to sing together in school was one thing. But why would Tyler ever choose to sing with her in front of the entire swim club?

Then, without warning, she found herself thinking about Jenna's comment about her third-grade trauma. She closed the journal. Cross-legged on her bed, Emily studied herself in the full-length mirror on the back of her door.

What she saw in the mirror was an ordinary girl, with summer-streaked brown hair, regular green eyes, and a face that wasn't totally embarrassing. What she was looking at, Emily realized, was the same girl who'd been told by a group of third graders on the playground, "You can't play with us anymore. We don't like you."

That was years ago, but the memory of it still made Emily's eyes fill with tears. Okay, so she'd been "sensitive." She still was. But was that a bad thing?

Back then, her dad had tried to make her feel better by saying, "They'll probably forget all about it tomorrow, and you'll be hanging out with them again. Besides, Em, it's only third grade. You kids are far too young to have cliques."

He might just as well have said, "Suck it up, Emily." But there *had* been cliques in elementary school. And being frozen out, for any reason, just plain hurt.

Was that why it was so important to her to include Aubrey in all their plans? Was LJ right? Was Emily playing Rescue Girl?

Well, so what if she was? They'd all agreed that Aubrey was fun and easy to be with. She fit in. She was a totally cool addition to their group. It didn't seem right to exclude her from LJ's party.

Her cell phone rang. Emily scrambled off the bed and pulled it out of her backpack. She checked caller ID — Jenna.

"Hey," Emily said, flipping the phone open. "I hope you're calling to tell me you talked your mom into inviting one more person. . . ."

"Nope. I deleted Sara, just like you said. LJ doesn't like her, and it's LJ's party, even if it's at my house. I just sent Aubrey an e-mail inviting her — and she was really psyched."

"Oh, Jen, that's great!"

"But unfortunately," Jenna added, "Tyler can't come."

"Oh," Emily said, surprised at how radically her stomach flipped with disappointment.

"Just kidding!" Jenna giggled. "He's coming. And he said, 'Emily's going to be there, right?'"

"He didn't!"

"No," Jenna confessed, enjoying her joke. "He didn't. But I bet he wanted to."

Even though Jenna couldn't see, Emily rolled her eyes.

For once, Jenna hadn't been exaggerating. Aubrey was thrilled about the party. She dove right in to helping Emily and Jenna plan and plot.

The next afternoon, while LJ was home helping her mom paint the kitchen, Aubrey showed up at the swim club bursting with excitement. She tracked down Emily and Jenna lounging by the pool.

"I've got the greatest idea," she announced. "I mean, I hope you'll like it."

"Spill," Jenna instructed, sitting up and turning all her attention to Aubrey.

"You know how you two were trying to come up with a theme for LJ's party?"

"And we couldn't and didn't," Emily sighed, laughing.

"Well, what if we made it an *American Idol*

party? I have a karaoke machine. I could bring it to your place, and everyone at the party could pick a song and audition. I'll run the machine, and you two and LJ can be the judges."

"Excellent!" Emily exclaimed. She and Aubrey looked at Jenna, who appeared to be giving the idea serious thought.

For a second, anyway.

That's all it took for Jenna to grin wildly and smush Aubrey and Emily in a group hug, totally forgetting her usual too-cool aura.

"Genius!" she shouted. "LJ can be Simon! Aubrey, that's an amazing idea!"

"What is?" Tyler and a couple of his friends had stopped to watch the trio's squeal fest. Emily flushed, embarrassed.

"Tyler, just the boy I wanted to see," Jenna said. "We're going to make LJ's surprise party an *American Idol* blowout. Isn't that genius?"

"Cute," Tyler said, smiling at Emily. He turned back to Jenna. "Cute idea."

"So will you try out?" Jenna asked. "You know, be one of the contestants at the party? We all know you're a good singer."

"Oh, Tyler!" Andy Mariani, one of Tyler's friends, said in a high-pitched voice. "Oh, please sing for us."

Tyler shoved Andy, laughing. "Sure," Tyler said, turning to Emily again. "If you'll sing with me at the club's talent show."

There was a moment of deafening silence in Emily's head, as if everything around her had stopped. Then she heard her heart race, and her own voice say, "Okay"— as if it were no big deal!

Chapter Five

❀

The Incredible
Disappearing Aubrey

Showers were predicted for the next two days. Sure enough, when Emily woke the next morning, it was to the ring of her cell phone and the pebbly rattle of rain against her window.

"Did I wake you?" Aubrey sounded like she'd been up for a while.

"No problem. What's up?"

"Want to go to the movies? It's totally cruddy out and that new Tony Shaw comedy, *The Boy Who Could,* opens today."

"Sure." Emily stifled a yawn and stretched her arms. "Hey, how's your mom?"

"My mom?" Aubrey sounded confused.

"Didn't you have to go to the doctor with her the other day? I'm sorry. I just thought something was wrong," Emily said.

"Oh," Aubrey said. "That. She's fine. She, uh, just wanted company. So should I call Jenna and LJ and find out if they're up for a movie?"

"That would be great. So you and your mom are really close, huh?" Emily noted.

She guessed that with all the moving around Aubrey's family had done, she must have developed some really tight bond with her mom. Emily had lived in Franklin Lakes for twelve and a half years. For her whole entire life.

"Yeah, we're kind of close," Aubrey said, moving on. "The movie starts at one o'clock. I'll call Jenna and LJ and meet you guys in the lobby at quarter of, okay?"

Emily paced between the popcorn stand and the wall of video games, glancing at her watch. LJ and Jenna had already gone into the theater. They'd said they would save two seats.

It was five minutes to one. Emily was torn between waiting for Aubrey, who might show up huffing and puffing any minute, or giving up and going to find her friends in the theater.

At 1:15, Emily gave up.

By the time she found LJ and Jenna in the dark, Emily had missed the beginning of the movie. The girls tried to fill her in, but they were shushed by annoyed people on either side of them.

At 2:15, during a tense moment in the movie, Emily's cell phone rang. Grumbles of frustration erupted all around her. Even Jenna hissed, "You're supposed to turn it off!"

Emily did. Then she rushed out of the theater, hoping the call hadn't been some sort of emergency from one of her parents.

It wasn't.

The message was from Aubrey. She sounded breathless, almost teary. She apologized a million times for not showing up, and she promised she'd explain when she met them for pizza after the show. Emily wasn't sure if she should be annoyed or worried.

"Nice going," Jenna told Aubrey, as she, Emily, and LJ slid into Aubrey's booth at California Pizza Kitchen. "We were practically tossed out of the movie because of your call —"

Aubrey's eyes widened. "But I thought Em's phone would be off. I only wanted to leave a message."

Emily knew she should be angry at Aubrey,

but the girl looked so genuinely sorry that Emily couldn't bring herself to give her the cold shoulder. "I forgot. I had it on because I thought you'd call, and when you didn't I rushed into the theater —"

"Fifteen minutes after the movie started!" LJ grumbled. She didn't have any trouble being annoyed, Emily noted.

"You guys, I am *so* sorry. It was . . . an emergency."

"Like your mom's dental and doctor appointments?" Jenna said. "Or did you have to unpack boxes again? Or go to your dad's base?" Jenna recounted all the "emergencies" that had made Aubrey leave early or show up late over the past few weeks.

"Is everything okay?" Emily asked anxiously. She knew Jenna was already worrying about Aubrey pulling a no-show at LJ's party, so she wasn't being very sensitive.

Embarrassed, Aubrey hung her head. When she lifted it again, her gray-green eyes were glossy with tears. "Please, please believe me. You have no idea how important you guys are to me —"

"You're important to us, too," Emily said.

Jenna rolled her eyes, but agreed. "Yeah. You are."

46

"So what was the crisis this time?" LJ asked.

Aubrey ducked her head again and studied CPK's huge menu. It was almost as if she were looking for an answer between the descriptions of the Hawaiian and New York Style pizzas. She did everything but squirm, and it looked to Emily like she'd do that in another second. "Nothing really," Aubrey mumbled into the menu. "I mean, nothing big. I just had to . . . meet my mom . . . again."

With more energy than necessary, Emily picked up her menu — even though she knew exactly what she'd order — and quickly changed the subject. "Anyway, you were right about *The Boy Who Could*," she said, forcing herself to sound cheerful. "It was awesome. So funny."

"And Tony Shaw is sooo cute," Jenna cut in.

"He really is. Did he look weird with blond hair?" Aubrey asked.

"What do you mean?" LJ asked, confused.

"I saw the previews. He has blond hair in the movie, right?" When LJ nodded, Aubrey added, "His real hair is almost black."

"Get out," LJ said. "For real?"

"How do you know what color his hair is?" Jenna asked, suspicious.

Emily saw a cloud of confusion pass across Aubrey's face. Her smile grew tentative.

"It was probably in some magazine," Emily offered. "Is that where you read it?"

"Oh, like I'd miss an article on someone as cool as Tony Shaw," Jenna scoffed.

"Actually, I know him," Aubrey said, not looking up from her menu. "What are you getting?" she asked Emily.

Three sets of jaws dropped. Aubrey knew a *movie star*?

For the first time since she'd met Aubrey, Emily wondered if her instincts about the girl were way off base. She'd always thought that Aubrey was totally real, good natured, and never so desperate for friends that she'd make stuff up. Except for her quick exits and supertight relationship with her mom, which, Emily had to admit, were kind of weird, she'd always had total confidence in her newest friend.

But now she was supposed to believe that Aubrey knew Tony Shaw and had never said a word about it? That was hard for Emily to wrap her mind around. Why would anyone play down such a juicy tidbit, if it were true?

"Wait a minute," she heard Jenna demand. "What do you mean, you *know* him?"

"Well, um, not exactly. I mean," Aubrey said,

finally looking up from the menu, "that I've met him. We go to the same . . . doctor. In the city —"

"New York City?" LJ said.

Aubrey nodded. "So what are you guys getting?"

"Not so fast," Jenna jumped in again. "You just moved to Franklin Lakes, and you and your mom already have a doctor in Manhattan?"

Emily decided to go with her gut. Aubrey wouldn't lie — unless it was absolutely necessary. Unless she was protecting a very important secret. *Her own*, Emily thought, *or someone else's*. "I'm getting the Thai Chicken pizza. What about you?" she asked Jenna.

"Same old, same old," Jenna replied. "So what's Tony Shaw really like?" she asked, turning back to Aubrey.

"Yeah, tell us all about what he's like in the waiting room — is he busy texting all the time, or reading scripts?" LJ teased.

"Tony? He seems really . . . patient," Aubrey responded slyly.

LJ picked up on it. "*Patient!* I get it."

"Ha-ha," Jenna grumbled.

"Yeah, that's *sick*," Emily joined in, poking Aubrey with her elbow.

"So are we ready to order?" Aubrey's good humor was restored. "What are you having, LJ?"

LJ pushed her menu away. "I'm not that hungry," she said. "Anyway, I'm babysitting the Terrible Twosome this afternoon. There's always lots to eat at their place."

It was the money, Emily knew. LJ had just spent a chunk of what she'd be earning today on the movie. She probably didn't want to blow more on pizza.

While Emily tried to think of a way to pay for LJ's food without insulting or embarrassing her friend, Aubrey stepped in.

"You know, I'm not that hungry, either. Want to share my pizza?" she asked LJ.

"Okay. Just a nibble, though," LJ said.

"What kind should we get?"

"The pepperoni's good," LJ noted, "or the Chipotle Chicken. It's hot and spicy. But get whatever you want."

When the waiter came to take their orders, Aubrey said, "I'll have the Chipotle Chicken. And an extra plate, please."

A wave of guilt crashed over Emily for doubting Aubrey, even for a minute. She caught the look that flickered from LJ to Aubrey, a look of grinning gratitude. And Emily's guilt was washed away — followed by the warm glow of pride.

As soon as LJ left to babysit, Aubrey said, "So what can I do to help with the party?"

"I think we've got everything covered," Emily said, leading her friends through the mall to the party store. She hoped they had it all covered, anyway. The party was less than a week away!

"Are you sure?" Aubrey looked so earnest, so eager to help — as if she had to make up for missing the movie.

"You're definitely bringing the karaoke machine, right?" Jenna asked. Aubrey nodded.

"I guess you could pick up the cake, too," Emily said. "The bakery's on your way to Jenna's."

Jenna cleared her throat. "Uh . . . not the best idea," she said. "If a new emergency popped up, we'd be birthday cakeless."

Aubrey looked hurt — for a moment. Then her bright smile was back. "I got LJ the best gift in the world," she said, changing the subject. "She's going to love it! So what are you guys wearing? I mean, what do most kids wear to parties around here? Dresses, jeans, something in between?"

"Sheesh," Jenna said, grinning, "haven't you ever been to a party before?"

"Well sure, but —" Aubrey blushed, then giggled. "I mean, I've worn so many fabulous clothes this summer, I just wouldn't know what to choose."

Emily laughed. "Right. Well, that's Jenna's department."

Jenna was laughing, too. "Lose the cargo pants," she said.

Chapter Six

❀

A Soldier at the Door

Jenna and Emily told LJ they were taking her out for an amazing dinner to celebrate her birthday.

"Dinner?" Predictably, LJ was not only surprised but obviously disappointed — just as Emily and Jenna knew she would be.

LJ had been looking forward to the blowout to end all blowouts this year, her most important birthday ever. This was the year when she'd be the first among them to become an official teen — her thirteenth birthday!

Emily could tell that LJ was trying to act like it was okay for her to have her over-the-top fantasy celebration be replaced by a quiet dinner with her two oldest friends. But it was obvious that she wasn't thrilled.

Emily and Jenna softened the blow by buying her an incredible birthday outfit, "to wear to the restaurant." LJ had drooled over the adorable red silk mini in Jenna's latest *Teen Vogue*. It would look fabulous with her glossy black hair and her sparkling dark eyes.

The birthday girl was scheduled to arrive at Jenna's at six-thirty on the night of her birthday. The rest of the party guests were supposed to be there, in the basement family room, at six–o'clock to get ready for the surprise.

LJ's dad had come to Jenna's house with some friends a few days earlier, to build a "stage" for the *American Idol* event. Jenna's dad had joined them, hauling his library desk downstairs. Jenna, LJ, and Emily were going to sit behind it to judge the contest. There were balloons everywhere — red, purple, and silver — and a huge "Happy Birthday, LJ!" sign that Emily's mom had painted. A long buffet table was set up on one side of the room, with platters of sandwiches, salads, ribs, wings, and tons of desserts.

Emily was looking for someplace to set down a bowl of chips, when she heard someone call out, "Tyler, over here!" She turned, expecting to see

Tyler coming down the stairs. Instead, he was right behind her, with a present in his hand. The bowl of potato chips she was holding jammed right into his ribs!

"Hey, thanks," he said. He grabbed a couple of chips.

Flustered, Emily backed up. "At least it wasn't the birthday cake," she heard herself say.

Tyler laughed. "Where do we put the presents?" he asked, as his friends Pete Hughes and Andy Mariani joined them.

"Over there," Pete answered. The boys walked off together — but not before Tyler grabbed another handful of chips and gave Emily a heart-melting grin.

By 6:15, everyone had shown up except the birthday girl herself, LJ's two sisters ... and Aubrey Foster.

When the doorbell rang, Jenna and Emily tore up the stairs, hoping it would be Aubrey and the karaoke machine.

They were half right. It was the karaoke machine, complete with CDs, a book of songs, and a birthday card from Aubrey.

Everything was handed over by a very young-looking soldier in dress uniform. "Are you Emily and Jenna, by any chance?" he asked.

"I am!" Jenna nearly shouted.

"She means *we are*," Emily corrected, trying not to laugh.

"Okay, great." The soldier pulled a piece of paper from his pocket, unfolded it, cleared his throat, and read: "Aubrey is sorry she'll be late tonight. She hopes that everything goes all right, and that all of you have an awesome night."

Emily blinked up at the soldier as he returned the poem to his pocket. He looked so relieved and proud that she almost expected him to take a bow.

Jenna shook her head, as if clearing it. "Um, maybe you'd like to come to our party?" she suggested, blushing wildly. "Ouch!" she added, when Emily pinched her arm.

The young soldier shrugged. "Sorry, ma'am. Gotta get back to the base." He turned and walked away down the front path.

"Yuck. He called me ma'am." Jenna looked like she'd sucked on a lemon. "That's what people call my *grandmother*! Emily, tell me the truth. Do I look like a ma'am?"

"No way," Emily assured her, holding the CDs and songbook. "He was just being polite."

Not totally satisfied, and grasping the karaoke machine, Jenna moved on. "I can't believe Aubrey pulled another no-show," she grumbled as they carried the equipment down to the party room.

Emily was surprised, too. Still, she felt a need to defend Aubrey. "Well, the guy said she was really sorry she couldn't make it —"

"Sorry? Really? That's new," Jenna said drily.

"— and that she'd try to get here as soon as possible," Emily continued. "At least she made sure the karaoke stuff showed up on time."

"Good thing none of us knows how to set it up," Jenna muttered as they reached the bottom of the stairs.

"I do," Andy Mariani volunteered.

Jenna looked up in surprise.

Emily stifled a giggle, watching her usually overconfident best friend brush a speck of imaginary lint off her top.

"That would be great," Jenna said to Andy. "Could you set up and run the karaoke machine tonight?"

Just then, LJ's sisters, Carmen and Sami, scooted in. Everyone had arrived, except for LJ.

And Aubrey.

Emily drifted over to the snack table. She couldn't figure it out. It was obvious that Aubrey liked hanging out with them — and vice versa. It was Aubrey who'd suggested the cool biking trip through the wildlife preserve. She'd also talked them into going to the beach instead of the swim club one afternoon. She'd brought along a Scrabble game, and even though Jenna and LJ had groaned about it at first, they'd all had a great time playing — even Jenna, whose face had gotten so burned that when she took off her sunglasses she'd looked like an owl.

Okay, so there was the movie incident and one other no-show, and a couple of weird quick exits. They were pretty much forgivable.

But how could Aubrey blow off LJ's thirteenth birthday party?

Jenna showed up at Emily's side, steaming.

"You're annoyed about Aubrey, right?" Emily asked.

"Oh, who cares?" Jenna scoffed.

But Emily knew better. Despite her sarcasm, Jenna had really come to like — even admire — Aubrey.

Except for her flaky disappearing act.

Other than that, Aubrey was easygoing and fun to hang out with and had some pretty cool ideas — like the *American Idol* party theme.

What Jenna felt now, Emily was willing to bet, wasn't really anger, so much as disappointment.

But Emily also knew that anger was easier to deal with. Disappointment hurt.

Chapter Seven

❀

LJ's Surprise

"Listen up, everyone. LJ's coming!" Jenna's mom called from the top of the stairs.

"Hide, hide!" Jenna hissed. Everyone but Jenna and Emily scattered. They ducked down behind sofas, chairs, and closet doors.

The doorbell rang. "LJ, happy birthday, sweetie. Wow, don't you look beautiful?" they could all hear Mrs. Lutz say. "Jenna and Emily are down in the family room. Go on, they're waiting for you."

"Oh, look at that sign." On her way down the stairs, LJ caught sight of the Happy Birthday banner Emily's mom had made. "Oh, guys," she called, "that was so nice of you. Thank —"

Before she could finish, LJ's sisters, friends, and classmates popped out from their hiding places, screaming, "Surprise!"

LJ froze. Her eyes opened wide, then flooded with tears.

"Dude, she's crying," Andy said, almost as stunned as LJ.

The laughter and shouting stopped suddenly as everyone stared at something that only Jenna and Emily had ever seen before. LJ Suarez, bright, beautiful, and tough as nails, was blubbering like a baby.

When the shock wore off, and LJ had been swarmed by her laughing, chattering friends, Emily explained that Aubrey had dreamed up the party theme — *American Idol*!

Emily and Jenna proudly showed LJ the stage that had been specially built for her party. It was set up against a wall, nearly dead center in the huge room. A couple of couches had been turned to face the stage.

Toward the front of the platform, in a tangle of wires, extension cords, and boxes, were Andy and Tyler, dutifully setting up the karaoke machine.

To their right, Jenna's father's big desk (the judges' table) was covered with purple pencils and pads of paper that had been inscribed "LJ's Big Thirteen!"

"So that we can make notes about the contestants," Jenna told LJ.

"And so everyone can write down which songs they want to sing," Emily added. "There are a bunch of notepads to give away as party favors, too. It was all Aubrey's idea."

LJ looked around the room. "Where is she?"

"Channeling her inner Houdini," Jenna said flatly.

"She's going to try to make it," Emily put in quickly. "And we're not going to do *American Idol* right this minute, anyway. Aubrey worked hard on the party, LJ. She'll probably be here soon."

"I hope so," LJ said, rushing to check out the karaoke songbook. "Or she'll miss out on the competition!"

Emily and Jenna watched as most of the boys drifted toward the pool table, leather sofas, and flat-screen TV on one side of the room. The girls, in groups of twos and threes, gathered near the food at the other end of the room.

The boys didn't actually play pool, Emily noted, and the girls didn't fill their plates. They all just stood around, occasionally glancing at one another.

"This is so not happening," Jenna mumbled miserably to Emily. "It's a disaster." She shook her head dramatically, sending a tumble of red curls flying.

We need music, Emily thought. But before she could say it aloud, a blast of sound came from the stage.

While Tyler duct-taped down the extension cords, Andy had popped one of Jenna's favorite songs into the karaoke player, and was rifling through the rest of her CDs.

The beat had a definite party-starter effect. Even though the boys and girls stayed on their own turf, several of them had, at least, begun to move to the music. Then Emily led a couple of girls over to the pool table, where, after a minute or two, they began kidding around with the boys. And Jenna called a couple of boys over to the food — where most of the girls had gathered.

The *American Idol* portion of the party was set for seven o'clock, after snacks but before cake. Unfortunately, so far, Emily's wish for Aubrey to show up remained just that — a wish.

During breaks in the music, while everyone was happily chowing down, Emily passed around the karaoke songbook. Almost all of the kids chose songs that they wanted to sing — some in groups, other gutsier ones solo.

When Emily showed the book to Tyler, he flipped through the pages and said, "Hey, here's the song we sang together in chorus. We could do this one, no problem."

"Problem," Emily said, blushing. "I'm one of the judges."

"Idea," Tyler countered. "How about we sing it for the swim club talent show instead?"

"Done deal," Emily said. She couldn't help the huge grin on her face.

By five to seven, Aubrey still hadn't shown. Emily and Jenna looked at their watches, then at each other.

Emily shrugged. Jenna shook her head. "It's time to start," she announced. "Anyway, Andy knows how to run the machine."

With LJ between them, they took their places behind Jenna's dad's desk. Everyone else piled onto the sofas and folding chairs set up around the stage.

Emily had the song list and order of appearance in front of her. Before she could call out Melissa Potter's name, though, Pete Hughes's friends pushed him onto the stage.

Andy rushed to find the song Pete was going to sing. Once he did, Pete *tried* to belt out Bruce Springsteen's "Magic"— but Jenna got the giggles, and Emily hid her smile behind her hands. "Um, nice try," she said, when he'd finished.

"Well, I guess we know who's playing Paula Abdul," LJ accused. Then she turned to Pete, her crush (though she'd never admit it to anyone but Emily and Jenna), and said, "No wonder you never made chorus. You're singing in the key of Not Even."

Everyone, even Pete, laughed.

"Ooooh," Jenna said. "Happy birthday, *Simon*."

"She's just kidding," Emily told Pete. "I give you a big thumbs-up for being the first to sing!"

The crowd loved it. They applauded wildly, as much for the judges as for Pete.

Melissa Potter, who could actually carry a tune, was up next. She was followed by Louise Bindler, who couldn't.

Then Jason Weiss sang. He earned his applause — and shrieks from the girls — more for how great he looked than how well he could sing. Which wasn't very well at all. Unfortunately, no one told him that as he butchered John Mayer's "No Such Thing."

Keisha Johnson did Jennifer Hudson's song,

"And I Am Telling You I'm Not Going" from *Dreamgirls,* and got the evening's wildest applause — until Tyler joined her for a duet from *High School Musical.* No contest, their performance earned the party's most ear-splitting shouts — and even a standing ovation!

At nine-thirty, Jenna's mom came downstairs carrying a chocolate birthday cake covered in white icing with pink sugar roses. Fourteen candles (one for good luck) burned on top of the cake.

Those who could do it well, and those who couldn't, all sang "Happy Birthday" to LJ.

"Still no Aubrey," Jenna muttered to Emily. "She totally blew us off."

Emily sighed. "She's got to have a good reason," she said, but she sounded uncertain, even to herself.

"Make a wish, make a wish," kids chanted at LJ.

Emily caught the sudden change in LJ's expression — from superpsyched to stressed. *There's so much going on*, Emily speculated, *I bet she can't decide what to wish for.*

Today was her birthday, her *thirteenth* birthday. Emily wanted to hug her and tell her that everything was changing.

LJ was an official teenager now.

She was starting junior high.

And just before the *Idol* contest, Pete Hughes had asked her to get pizza with him sometime.

Maybe wishes made on such a special occasion counted more than everyday wishes. For LJ's sake, Emily hoped so.

And it looked like LJ did, too, as she finally blew out the candles.

While Emily and Jenna handed out slices of cake, LJ announced that Keisha and Tyler were the clear *Idol* winners.

Her announcement was met with cheers of agreement. No contest!

Eventually, the party broke up, with everyone complimenting LJ, Emily, and especially Jenna for throwing the best bash ever.

"The *American Idol* theme was so cool!" declared Hannah Hopkins, who prided herself on having been the pop culture critic for *The Franklinian*, their one-page elementary school newspaper.

Jason Weiss, still stunned by what a good time he'd had, said, "Hey, thanks for inviting me. It was a lot of fun."

"That karaoke machine was the best!" Keisha Johnson exclaimed.

Emily was flushed, in part from all the compliments; in part from running around, making sure everything went off without a hitch; in part because her shouted comments about the *Idol* contestants had left her laughing, wired, and winded.

But the best part was that the party had really surprised and touched LJ, and had been a whopping success with everyone else.

A moment later, Emily watched Tyler head upstairs to go home. When he was halfway up the steps, he turned and ran back down. "I'll call you soon to talk about the swim club talent show, okay, Taylor?" Emily couldn't help grinning at how he called her by her last name.

Jenna stepped in front of Emily, who was temporarily speechless. "Totally okay," she assured him. Tyler grinned, and disappeared up the stairs.

"You guys," LJ gushed, running over to them. "You're the absolute best. I just wish Aubrey had been here, too, to see how well the *Idol* thing went over —"

"Aubrey! I almost forgot." Emily rushed over to

the gift table piled with ribboned boxes and colorful shopping bags. "She sent you a card."

"A card?" Jenna rolled her eyes. "How special."

"Actually," Emily said, handing the envelope to LJ, "she said it was the perfect present. Let's see."

LJ tore open the envelope. Inside was a beautiful beaded and sequined card, which Aubrey had clearly made herself. "It's so sweet," LJ said. Then she opened the card and her dark eyes widened. Her face went white. She forced herself to take a deep breath. "Is it real?" she whispered.

"What?" Jenna asked, edging in to look over LJ's shoulder.

"I'm sure it is real," Emily said softly, as if the normal sound of her voice might disintegrate the gift.

"Five tickets," LJ told Jenna. "For the three of us, Aubrey, and my mom. Look!" LJ was close to tears for the second time that day. "Tickets to the Summer Fest concert at Madison Square Garden!"

Chapter Eight

❊

No-Show

The next morning, Emily, Jenna, and LJ were surrounded as soon as they showed up at the swim club. Kids couldn't stop talking about the party!

Those who'd been there thanked them for the invitations and said — again — what a great time they'd had; those who hadn't said they'd heard all about it and asked if they could please, please be invited next time.

Emily, LJ, and Jenna (whose pale, freckled face, Emily noted, was positively aglow with party success) were chatting happily when a murmur rippled through the crowd. People parted like the Red Sea to let Sara Livingston through.

The wide smile of triumph froze on Jenna's face. But the glow disappeared.

"Hi, there," Sara said, fluttering her navy blue nails at them. "Sorry I couldn't make it to your . . . adorable little party. Oops!" She clapped her palm over the phony O she'd made with her lips. "That's right. I wasn't invited, was I?"

Impossible as it seemed to Emily, Jenna's face turned even whiter.

"But I heard a rumor that I *was* on the guest list . . . until I was taken off to make room for someone *who never even showed up.*" Sara smirked. "Bad move."

Some of the crowd giggled nervously. Others began to drift away —*Though "skulk away" is more like it,* Emily thought.

"Who told you that?" Emily demanded.

"Oh, I've got my sources," Sara said archly.

"Sources?" LJ challenged, glaring. "Spies, you mean."

"Like *I* need spies?" Sara scoffed. "My mom and I were in the city, taking in a *fabulous* Broadway show. And who should I see outside at intermission but your dear friend, Aubrey."

"Aubrey went to a play last night?" LJ asked.

"Oh, no. She was just hanging out in the city . . . *with her mother*! On a Saturday night."

"Just like you were?" LJ pointed out.

"She got you," Melissa Potter chimed in from the crowd.

Sara ignored her. "Imagine how surprised I was. Aubrey, the girl who was supposed to replace me at the party, seemed to be having a great time without any of you. Just like me."

Jenna tossed her head. "We knew she wasn't going to show. She sent over the most adorable soldier to tell us. He wanted to join us, but —"

"But we already had the perfect mix of guests," LJ cut in. "The perfect mix — without you."

"Oooh, low blow," another girl said, giggling.

Sara spun toward the girl, staring daggers.

"Hi, guys." Suddenly all eyes (including Sara's) were on Aubrey, who had just walked up. "Um, what's going on?"

"Don't say anything," Emily told her. "You don't have to say anything. Not here."

"Oh, you guys." Aubrey turned to her friends, her eyes wide. "I'm *so* sorry I didn't show up last night. My mom and I went into the city —"

Sara's jaw dropped. Emily could tell she never expected Aubrey to come out with the truth.

Aubrey didn't even glance in Sara's direction. "It was an emergency. An absolute emergency. I'd never have gone, otherwise. You guys know how excited I was about the party."

Sara had to have the last word, even if it was totally unrelated. "Don't even think about winning the swim club talent show. You don't stand a chance." With that, she turned and stalked away.

"Okay, so what really happened to you last night?" Jenna asked, ignoring Sara's comment, as soon as the crowd around them dispersed.

Aubrey sighed. "I had an appointment. It was really important, and came up at the last minute — and ran way overtime. I thought I could catch the tail end of LJ's party, but I was stuck. Did the karaoke machine get there on time, at least?"

"It was all ready when I showed up," LJ assured her.

"Were you surprised?" Aubrey asked hopefully.

"Shocked. Stunned. And the karaoke machine was totally fun. But the *tickets*!" LJ squealed. "I couldn't believe it. How did you get them?"

"It was no big deal," Aubrey said. "There are some perks to being in a military family. We get offered free or discount tickets to concerts, plays, sporting events, all sorts of things in whatever city we're closest to."

"That's amazing!" Jenna exclaimed. "It's definitely *my* favorite birthday present that LJ has ever gotten."

Aubrey just smiled.

By mid afternoon, the sun was blazing overhead. Even the pool couldn't cool the girls off. Especially since they had to huddle at the shallow end, where the younger kids splashed and screamed, while a crew of high school guys headbutted a soccer ball around in the deeper water.

Emily glanced up at the lifeguard chair. Tyler wasn't there.

"I am so out of here," Jenna declared after a few minutes. "Let's find some shade."

"There's plenty at the Snack Shack. And maybe you" — LJ turned to Emily, grinning — "can chill in Tyler's shadow."

"Is he there?" Emily whispered, as the girls climbed out of the pool. Her face suddenly felt sunburned.

"Like you didn't notice," Jenna said.

"Did he call you about the talent show yet?" LJ asked.

"Oh, please," Emily said. "It hasn't even been twenty-four hours since he said he would."

"But who's counting?" LJ asked with mock innocence.

"Are you really going to ditch us to do a duet with him?" Jenna demanded. "We can't exactly be a trio without you."

"I think I'm a few beats behind." Aubrey followed Emily across the grass. "Are you officially going to sing with Tyler at the swim club talent show?"

"Yeah. I mean, we're supposed to talk about it."

"Oh, Em," Aubrey said softly. "That would be so perfect."

"It really would," Emily whispered back. "But I'm not sure it's definite."

"It will be," Aubrey said, grinning. "Trust me."

"Excuse me?" Jenna caught the last phrase and turned around to face Aubrey. "Trust you? Based on what?" she said snidely.

"Fair enough." Aubrey's feelings were hurt. Emily could hear it in her voice and see it on her face. She thought Aubrey might say more, but she didn't. Instead, she tossed back her long dark hair, still damp from the pool, and gulped, as if swallowing a bitter pill.

Quick, change the subject, Emily's inner voice commanded. She didn't like Aubrey's weird disappearing act, but she could feel Aubrey's embarrassment as if it had just happened to her.

In fact, it *had* happened to her, when she was seven years old.

In third grade, Emily had been part of a small group of girls led by Sara Livingston, who was bossy even back then.

One day, Emily arrived at school and Sara blurted out that she was no longer part of their group. Then she and her friends turned their backs and went back to playing.

Emily's heart began to pound like crazy, pulsing all the way up through her ears. She wanted to run away, but she couldn't move her feet. Her heart pumped even faster than before. Stars danced in front of her eyes.

"Why?" was all she managed to squeak out.

"Because you got cooties!" Sara retorted, glancing at Emily over her shoulder and sticking her tongue out. Her little friends laughed.

"She does not!" someone hollered. It was LJ. Her raven-black hair was short then; her long, tan legs notched with knobby knees. She hurried to Emily's side and called back to Sara, "We don't like you, either."

Sara gasped.

Jenna (who Emily really liked, partly because she looked like a red-haired Muppet) came over next.

"Cooties?" Jenna said to Sara. "Takes one to know one."

The comebacks weren't brilliant, but they did the trick. The three of them walked away and never looked back.

But every once in a while, the ugly memory returned with brute force. And now, Emily experienced that same kind of embarrassment and helplessness again — in Aubrey.

"Idea," Emily said, stopping and turning to Aubrey. "Why don't *you* sing with Jenna and LJ? Then they could still be part of a trio. Just in case Tyler really does want to sing with me."

Jenna looked ready to challenge her friend but, instead, turned toward Aubrey — and gave her a deliberate once-over. Emily could practically read Jenna's mind. And the little smile that stole across Jenna's face confirmed exactly what Emily was thinking.

Ever since they were little, Jenna had loved to play dress up. She'd pull costumes out of her closet (and sometimes her mother's) and Emily and LJ would model them, tottering on heels that were way too high and too big for them.

Once in a while, Jenna would raid her mom's makeup drawer. She'd haul out a jumble of foundations, powders, lipsticks, eyeliners, blush, and whatever else she could find. Then she'd make up their faces, and usually insist that they all paint their toes and fingernails.

At some point (Emily couldn't remember when), she and LJ had decided that they were too old for the game.

If Emily was right, Jenna Lutz had found just what she'd been wishing for since then — a living, breathing doll to play dress up with. And her name was Aubrey.

"Can you sing?" Jenna asked abruptly. Aubrey nodded.

"Yeah, but can you really, *really* sing?" LJ added. "I want to win this contest."

"I take singing lessons," Aubrey said, shyly. She looked more like she'd betrayed a secret, Emily noted, than that she'd shared a qualification.

LJ grinned, but Jenna wasn't done yet. "Can you dance, too?"

"I think so. I mean, okay, I also take dance." There it was again — more an admission of guilt than something to brag about.

LJ looked psyched. Jenna? Not so much. Emily knew she was thinking about the downside: What if Aubrey got one of her mysterious, urgent calls the day of the contest? What if she leaped off the stage in the middle of their number or, even worse, never made it to the show? It wouldn't be that unlikely.

"Sounds good," LJ suddenly announced. "Let's do it."

"We can give it a shot," Jenna said, less certain.

"Oh, thanks, you guys!" Aubrey squealed. "We'll be awesome, I promise."

"Promise? Don't even bother," Jenna grumbled. They'd reached the shade of the Snack Shack. Tyler was there, standing between Skyler Moore and Blake O'Brien, two of the iciest of Sara Livingston's Ice Queens.

Emily didn't have the nerve to just walk over to Tyler, especially now, but she was close enough to hear Blake whining, "Oh, but Ty, why not? We'd make the best group."

Tyler didn't say anything; he just sipped his drink and smiled.

He forgot! Emily realized. Her stomach fell like a broken elevator. Tyler had forgotten that he'd asked *her* to sing with him.

"You know, I'm really talented," Skyler said, not giving up. "I was in the school play last year, remember? And everyone said I was awesome —"

"Everyone in your family," LJ muttered in passing.

Skyler heard her and did a decent imitation of Sara's death-ray squint.

"Hey, Taylor," Tyler called to Emily. "Got a minute? I'm back on duty in five."

"Um, okay," Emily said.

"Sorry, guys," Tyler told the blonds. "Gotta go." He tossed his drink cup into the trash and walked over to Emily. "So?" he said.

"So?" she repeated.

"I still think that the duet from chorus would really work for the talent show. We've already got it down, so it wouldn't take much practice."

Elevator up! Emily glanced over at her friends. They were listening intently, but when she turned toward them, they got busy talking to one another. Except for Aubrey, who looked right at Emily and Tyler and said, "What an excellent idea. You guys would be great together."

"See?" Tyler said.

Emily shot Aubrey a grateful smile. Then she took a deep breath and turned back to Tyler. "Okay. Let's do it," she said.

Nearby, Blake gasped. She couldn't help herself. "We are in so much trouble," she said. "Sara is *not* going to like this."

Later that afternoon, the girls gathered at Emily's house to talk about the talent show. Jenna, LJ, and Aubrey were still trying to figure out what their act would be.

Aubrey sat cross-legged on Emily's pink reading chair. LJ and Emily were perched on the white four-poster bed. Jenna was studying herself in Emily's full-length mirror. She finally turned to face her friends. "I was thinking we could do 'Irreplaceable,' by Destiny's Child. I could be Beyoncé," she said.

"'Irreplaceable'?" Emily snorted. "Jenna, that song is a Beyoncé solo. It doesn't even include the other two girls!"

"What if we did a song by the Dixie Chicks? That's three girls, and I could be Natalie Maines," LJ suggested.

"Except you're not short and blond," Jenna reminded LJ.

"Oh, like you're Beyoncé's double?" LJ shot back.

"Wait, I've got an idea," Aubrey said excitedly. "What if we do something like that song from

Hairspray, 'You Can't Stop the Beat'?" All the girls had seen the movie, and that was their favorite number.

Jenna bit her lip. "I don't know how convincing we'd be."

"*That* is what costumes are for!" Aubrey declared. "I can dress up as Edna, the mom. LJ, you can be Tracy, the star, and Jenna, you can be Penny, the blond best friend.

Emily was amazed. In one sweeping gesture, Aubrey had resolved everything.

"'You Can't Stop the Beat' is in the karaoke songbook!" Emily remembered.

"Which means," Aubrey pointed out, "that we'd have a built-in backup band!"

"Listen," Jenna said, suddenly serious. "This contest means a lot to me and LJ. Especially since Sara thinks she can take it away from us."

"The only way that would happen is if the Ice Queens do a scene from *The Wizard of Oz,* and Sara plays the Wicked Witch," Emily said.

"Now that would be typecasting," LJ agreed, laughing.

Chapter Nine

❁

You Can't Stop It

The girls were eager to start rehearsals. While they wolfed down burgers and mini Caesar salads at the Snack Shack the next afternoon, Aubrey offered to bring the karaoke machine to Jenna's or LJ's place, if it was more convenient for practicing.

"Rehearsing at LJ's is out of the question," Jenna said.

"Yeah," LJ agreed. "My little sisters would never leave us alone. And your mom" — she nodded to Jenna — "would probably force-feed us carrots and celery every five minutes if we rehearsed at your house."

"She's this compulsive hostess." Jenna sighed. "All about nutrition, too."

"Well, if you don't mind unpacked boxes, ladders, and rolled-up rugs, we can rehearse at my place this afternoon," Aubrey piped up.

"Great!" Emily quickly backed Aubrey's suggestion. She had to admit, she was curious about where their new friend lived and what life was like in a military family. "I'll come along — and bring my *Hairspray* DVD."

An hour later, after they'd stopped by Emily's house for the DVD, the four friends rode their bikes to Aubrey's. She hadn't been kidding about it being a still-getting-settled booby trap. No one would have guessed it from the outside of Aubrey's house. But inside, Emily wouldn't have been surprised if Aubrey's mom had handed them construction helmets in order to make it safely up the stairs.

"Don't even look around down here," Aubrey warned, as they picked their way past mounds of books, paintings, and boxes. "My room's pretty much set up," she added, leading the way upstairs.

It was, Emily was relieved to see. Set up, sunny, and fun. As Aubrey and LJ flipped through the karaoke songbook to find "You

Can't Stop the Beat," Emily and Jenna checked out the cool posters and photos plastered on the walls.

Emily noticed a framed picture of Aubrey, grinning her big, white smile and holding up a tube of Good-to-Glow toothpaste. It was amazing how much it looked like a real ad.

Aubrey looked amazing in the photo. Her dark hair was glossy and full; subtle makeup highlighted her gorgeous gray-green eyes.

Jenna peered at the photo over Emily's shoulder. "Is that you, Aubrey? I mean, is it for real?"

LJ came over and studied it.

Aubrey didn't look happy about the discovery, Emily noticed. In fact, she looked kind of embarrassed — as if she'd gotten caught with something she wasn't supposed to have.

Before Aubrey could say anything, LJ rolled her eyes and said, "Oh, please, Jenna. I have one just like it. You know that shot of me and my sisters on the cover of *Teen People*? It's a setup. You go to get your picture taken, and they can make it look like you're on the cover of any magazine you want." Aubrey just nodded and turned back to the karaoke machine.

That seemed to settle it — for LJ and Jenna, anyway. For some reason, Emily wasn't convinced. The whole setup looked so professional, especially Aubrey's makeup. It wasn't like the little bit of makeup Emily had noticed on her friend at the beach. In this shot, Aubrey's features were brighter, bolder, more colorful. And her hair, usually a cute but casual mess, gleamed flawlessly.

"Pssst!" As Aubrey and LJ fiddled with the controls on the karaoke machine, Jenna whispered, "Em, take a look at this."

Under a pile of notebooks, Jenna had found the front cover of a playbill, the pamphlet given out at a show that listed who was who in the cast and crew.

The single page was from *The Secret Garden*, a musical based on a book both Jenna and Emily had always loved. The cover of the playbill showed a girl standing beside a garden gate. Although the girl's dark hair was much shorter than Aubrey's, and the shot was small and grainy, the garden-gate girl looked an awful lot like their new friend.

"The toothpaste photo was fake," Jenna whispered authoritatively. "But this? This is the real thing."

"Got it!" Aubrey called out, waving the CD featuring the background music and lyrics to the *Hairspray* finale.

"Hey, what are you guys looking at?" LJ came over and examined the playbill. "Wow! Is that you, Aubrey?"

"It is. Or was," Aubrey responded, almost reluctantly. *The girl must have had a brag-ectomy*, Emily thought. Her need for praise and attention were definitely missing in action.

"I was in that play when we lived in Texas. I was ten, the only kid on the base who could sing well enough to play the part." Aubrey looked embarrassed.

"So it was a military production?" Jenna asked.

Aubrey nodded. She looked trapped. LJ didn't even notice. "How cool," she enthused. "I'm so glad you're going to sing with us!"

"Yeah, and I'm so glad *you guys* thought of it," Emily joked.

"Have you ever considered wearing your hair short again?" Jenna studied Aubrey. "It looks really cute in the picture. I have the best hairdresser. Maybe we could go tomorrow! I could tell him exactly what to do."

"That's so sweet, Jenna. Only I really can't."

"Can't, or won't?" Jenna put one hand on her hip.

"Can't," Aubrey repeated. "Not tomorrow,

anyway. Not until the fall, I don't think. But thanks. It's a cool idea."

"Don't judge by my hair," Jenna said quickly. "I mean, it looks really great after he styles it, it's just hard to tame — especially in the summer."

"I like your hair," Aubrey responded, grinning.

"Watch out, Sara Livingston," LJ cackled, waving the playbill cover in the air. "We *Hairspray* girls have a secret weapon. A real child star."

"Why didn't you tell us?" Jenna asked. "I mean, if I'd been in any musical, ever, I would have told the world."

"More like the universe," Emily cracked.

"So tell the truth," LJ urged. "Were you in other plays? Other musicals? Were you ever in *Hairspray*?"

Aubrey shook her head. "Nope. Or, not yet, anyway," she teased, pushing PLAY on the karaoke machine.

After watching Emily's DVD, Jenna, LJ, and Aubrey played the last *Hairspray* song over and over again, listening carefully. Aubrey was all about authenticity. She'd been really serious about wanting to dress the part and get every dance move down.

"I'm totally right for the part of Penny!" Jenna declared. "But I think Aubrey should be Tracy." Tracy was the star of the movie.

Aubrey disagreed. It seemed clear to Emily that she didn't want to be in the spotlight. But why not?

"It's got to be LJ. Come on, you know you want to be a star," Aubrey teased.

LJ laughed. "But you probably have the best voice. You should be front and center."

"You haven't even heard me sing yet," Aubrey protested. "And besides, I've always wanted to be a girl playing a guy playing a middle-aged woman. I'll be Tracy's mom, Edna. It'll be fun."

As far as Jenna was concerned, as long as she got to be Penny, it was settled. "Okay, so LJ, you're Tracy, and Aubrey can be Edna."

First, they had to memorize all the words. Even though they intended to use the karaoke machine during the talent show, Jenna was sure that they wouldn't be able to read the lyrics while they were dancing. "We'll totally get more votes if we look professional," she decreed.

From her perch on the comfy, oversized armchair next to Aubrey's desk, Emily shook her head. "Good luck with that," she called out. "Do you guys even realize how many verses that song has? There are a lot more than just the chorus."

They found out soon enough.

The threesome bunched behind the karaoke machine, staring at the small monitor. As the song lyrics rolled by, they sang along, trying to memorize the exact words. *All* of them.

"How many different verses are there?" LJ was starting to sound worried. "Every time I think we're done, a new one starts."

Not surprisingly, the girls didn't nail the song the first time — or the second, third, or fourth.

One or another of them always blew it, forgetting or messing up a line. LJ kept tripping over "The motion of the ocean or the sun in the sky." Instead, she sang, "An ocean of emotion."

Jenna, who had been confident that their rehearsal would be a breeze, fumbled on several lines. The one that gave her the most trouble was "You can wonder if you wanna, but I never ask why."

Jenna sang it wrong so many times that Aubrey pointed playfully at her and sang loudly, "You can *blunder* if you wanna . . ."

Jenna then planted herself right in front of the screen, jostling Aubrey out of the way. She sang the line correctly, then turned to Aubrey, her eyes squinted, her hands held like claws. "Heh, heh, heh, my pretty," she screeched in a witchy voice. "You will totally mess up, too."

LJ covered her mouth, trying not to laugh.

A mischievous sparkle lit up Aubrey's eyes. Emily could tell that she had something up her sleeve.

When the music started again, Aubrey jumped in front of the screen. Instead of going after Jenna, she turned to LJ and sang, "You can't stop the *Pete*."

Overtired and giddy, everyone cracked up.

It was on!

Jenna, LJ, and Aubrey raced to one-up each other. They pushed and wriggled to get in front of the screen, read the words, and think of something silly to replace them with.

Their substitutions were ridiculous, and they knew it. They came up with gems like "You can't stop to eat . . . to cheat . . . your feet." All the while, they laughed, bumped, and careened into one another.

The madness was contagious. Emily had no idea what came over her. Before she realized what she was doing, she bolted up and jumped in front of her three friends, blocking the screen, and sang, "And you guys are dead meat!"

LJ hit her with a ruffled pillow from Aubrey's bed. Emily returned the favor with an old stuffed teddy bear. Before long, they were in the middle of an all-out, throw-anything-soft-you-can-find fight, until the girls collapsed on the bed, laughing so hard that tears ran down their faces.

Jenna tried to pull herself together. She rolled over to face Emily, who was still giggling.

"You know," Jenna said, "there's no rule that says you can only be part of one act. Maybe you should sing with us, too. Practically the whole cast sings that song in the end." Jenna scooted to the edge of the bed and stood up. Giving Aubrey an impish grin, she added, "You know, just in case Aub pulls a no-show."

This time, Aubrey didn't flinch. Still giggling, she got off the bed and deliberately hip-checked Jenna, who pretended to be seriously wounded and staggered backward. "Cut it out. We really need to work," Jenna gasped in mock-seriousness.

Aubrey's deliberate goofiness had started it, and now they were all having a great time. For a second, Emily was almost tempted to take Jenna up on her offer and sing with them.

Then she thought of Tyler. She was already nervous enough about their number! Adding another performance to the mix definitely wouldn't help, no matter how much fun the rehearsals were.

Just then, LJ's cell phone rang. She checked the caller ID and groaned, "It's the twins' mom. I know she's going to want me for Tuesday, but I promised to take my sister, Carmen, to see *The Boy Who Could*. She's crazy about Tony Shaw, and my parents won't let her go alone."

"Ugh." Jenna shook her head. "What a bummer."

"Can't you take your sister to the movie tomorrow?" Emily asked.

"No. *She's* babysitting tomorrow. And Tuesday is the last day it's playing here."

As LJ answered the call, Emily glanced over at Aubrey. She looked like her brain was sprinting on a hamster wheel. "What're you thinking?" Emily asked her.

"Just trying to figure something out," Aubrey responded.

"She's hooked and booked." Jenna sighed. She'd been listening to LJ's half of the call.

LJ confirmed it when she got off the phone, groaning. "I told her I'd do it. It's a whole afternoon, from twelve to five, and she pays more than double what the other moms do."

"But what about your sister?" Aubrey asked.

"She'll understand." LJ shrugged. "In a year or two."

"What time's the show?" Aubrey wanted to know.

"It starts at one," LJ told her. "Why?"

"Idea," Aubrey said, the way Emily usually did. Aubrey acknowledged Emily with a wink. "What if I fill in for a few hours while you take Carmen to the movie? I've babysat before — how hard could it be?"

LJ took a minute to think it over. Then her hopeful smile melted into an unhappy frown. "I wish, but these are the Lasky twins we're talking about," she said. "They're not your average mini-monsters."

"Idea," Emily added. "What if I go with Aubrey? Then it would be two against two. Better odds."

"I'd go, too," Jenna said, "but my mom and I are going into the city on Tuesday. I have to get some gross bridesmaid dress for my cousin's wedding."

"That's okay," Aubrey said. "Em and I can probably handle it. What do you think, LJ?"

"That would be so cool. Are you sure?" LJ looked at Aubrey and Emily, who both nodded. "You'd really do that?"

As the girls turned back to practicing, the sun began to fade outside. After a while, the elated trio had most of the song lyrics down and no longer needed to watch the karaoke monitor — they could concentrate on the moves.

Best of all, Emily noted, Aubrey's mom hadn't interrupted, beeped, texted, or called her once. Miracle.

At home that night, Emily found herself thinking about Mrs. Foster again — Mrs. *Captain* Foster, she had to remind herself.

Emily was in her pj's, curled up in her pink armchair, when a horrible thought crossed her mind. She put down the book she'd been reading and tried to remember all the times Aubrey had been called away to do something with her mother.

She called Jenna. "Jen, I just had a terrible thought."

"Me, too," her friend responded. "What if Pete joins up with Blake and Skyler for the talent show? You know how desperate they were to latch onto a boy for their act. LJ would be so mad!"

"Jenna, this is important," Emily said, trying to hide her irritation.

"Oh, like having the Ice Queens steal Pete for their frosty act isn't?"

"Jen, what if Aubrey's mom is sick?"

"You know, I've been thinking the same thing. There's something seriously ill about the way she checks up on Aubrey all the time and has to know where she is every minute —"

"I mean sick, as in *sick*," Emily interrupted. "What if she has some serious illness and has to go to the doctor in the city for . . . treatments?"

"Treatments?" Jenna echoed. "You think Aubrey's mom is really sick?"

"I don't know. But it would explain a lot, wouldn't it?"

Jenna suddenly sounded upset. "Oh, I hope not."

There was a beep on Emily's line. "Hold on," she said to Jenna. "I've got another call coming in."

Emily checked caller ID. The number was familiar. It took a minute before she realized why.

Tyler Cunningham was calling her!

Emily's heart raced. Flustered, she checked the mirror to see if her hair looked okay — even though Tyler couldn't see her over the phone.

Emily willed herself to take a deep breath before answering the call.

"Hi, Tyler," she said in a borderline squeaky voice.

"Hey, Taylor. Listen, Tuesday is my day off. We're having dinner with my grandma that night, but I'm free in the afternoon. Want to start rehearsing for the talent show?"

"That would be awesome!" Emily exclaimed. Then she remembered the babysitting job. Oh, no! *Maybe Aubrey can handle it herself?* she thought desperately. Not from what Emily knew of the twins. *Maybe Jenna could take my place?* But no, Jenna was going into the city with her mom.

Emily couldn't find an out. "My bad," she told Tyler. "I forgot I have to babysit Tuesday afternoon. I'm helping LJ out."

"Oh." Emily couldn't help noticing that Tyler sounded disappointed. She was thrilled that he cared, but suddenly scared that he'd think the whole idea of them singing together was too complicated, not worth it.

"Okay, we'll get started another time — but soon," he said, surprising her. "So what're you up to?"

Emily smiled shyly, glad they weren't face-to-face. She could feel her cheeks warm and knew that she was blushing.

Then she remembered Jenna. "Yikes. I'm so sorry, I've got to go. I have a call on the other line."

Emily wanted to kick herself as soon as the words left her mouth. Why had she said that? Why didn't she just tell Jenna she'd call her back? She'd made it sound like someone more important than Tyler was on the other line.

"Okay." Tyler seemed thrown. "I guess I'll see you."

"Absolutely," Emily said, as upbeat as possible. "Probably tomorrow."

Chapter Ten

Secrets

"It's possible," LJ said the next day at the swim club, when Emily shared her theory about Aubrey's mom. "If you're right, that would be terrible."

They were sitting on the steps in the shallow end of the pool. Emily glanced over her shoulder to make sure that Aubrey was still in line at the Snack Shack.

"Hey, I've got a crazy idea," LJ added, with a hint of sarcasm. "Why don't we ask her?"

"I'll tell you why," Jenna announced, in her official daughter-of-the-doctor voice. "Some people don't like to talk about things like that. My dad says he sees it at the hospital all the time. You have to respect the patients' wants, as well as their needs."

"I guess you're right," Emily said. "But don't you think most people would want their friends to be there for them? It doesn't seem right that Aubrey should have to face a situation like this alone."

"Alone?" Jenna was eyeing the Snack Shack. "How about with Jason Weiss and Reef Marmon?"

Emily turned. Jason was on one side of Aubrey, and Reef was on the other. Aubrey walked back toward Emily and the girls, juggling not one, but four water bottles — one for herself and three for her friends.

Emily was touched — again — by Aubrey's easy thoughtfulness. As she made her way toward the pool, Reef took the bottles of water from Aubrey's left hand, as if they were a burden too heavy for her to handle.

Jason gave him a nasty look and tried to get the two remaining bottles from Aubrey's right hand — but Reef reached for them, too.

Aubrey's 45 SPF sunblock, Emily noticed,

couldn't prevent the burning blush that reddened her face.

As she neared the pool, Aubrey took the bottles back. "Thanks a lot, you guys," she said. "See you later, okay?"

Jason and Reef both stood there for a minute. Neither of them, Emily realized, wanted to be the first to leave.

LJ cleared her throat. "See you later," she repeated emphatically to the boys.

The boys seemed to snap out of their trance. Jason headed back to the Snack Shack, and Reef trotted toward the volleyball court.

"Do you like them?" LJ asked Aubrey, accepting a water bottle. "Do you, you know, *like* either one of them?"

"They're both really nice," Aubrey said. "But no —"

"She's all crushed out on Tony Shaw, right?" Jenna said.

"He's really cute," Emily put in. "I read that he's doing some new TV series this fall."

"I heard that, too," Aubrey said quietly.

"So what's going on with your mom?" Jenna asked abruptly, accepting the bottled water Aubrey handed her.

"Jenna!" LJ was stunned. "What about what you just said?"

"I didn't say it, my dad did," Jenna said defensively.

Aubrey looked rattled by the question. "What are you talking about?" she asked.

"You've got to excuse Jenna. She's got a blurting disorder." Emily stood up. "Let's go for a walk on the beach," she suggested.

"I think I'll pass," LJ decided. "I'm going to check out the volleyball game."

"Me, too." Jenna stood up and shook her head like a wet golden retriever. Water sprayed from her red explosion of hair. Surprised by the sudden shower, Emily and Aubrey shrieked and jumped back. Jenna waved at them and called over her shoulder, "Later!"

"What was that all about?" Aubrey asked, as she and Emily walked toward the club's small strip of sand. "The thing about my mom?"

Emily shrugged. She wanted to know the truth about Aubrey's mom and possibly help her friend. But on the other hand, she didn't want to push Aubrey to reveal something she might not want to talk about, something that could possibly hurt or embarrass her.

They hit the warm sand, and Emily, barefoot, headed toward the lake. Aubrey got one flip-flop off and hopped after her.

"Emily." Aubrey stopped short and took Emily's arm. "What's going on?" she demanded, bending to remove her other shoe. She tossed both flip-flops into the sand. "I hate being left out. Come on, what did Jenna mean?"

"Um, well," Emily began. "I think I started it. I was thinking about all the times you've kind of disappeared. And it's always with your mom. And then you come back with these, I hate to say it, but kind of lame excuses."

Aubrey looked away. "I'm sorry. You have no idea how rotten I feel about that." She was staring out at the lake. What Emily could see of her profile — sad, upset — half-convinced her that she'd been right. Was there really something wrong with Aubrey's mother?

"Oh, Em, my mom is totally fine. I wish I could tell you what's actually up. I've been dying to tell someone."

Emily just waited. Finally, Aubrey turned to face her again. "You especially," she said. "I've been wanting to talk to you about it almost since we met. But I can't. I can't take the chance. Soon, I hope."

"Nice," Emily said, trying to lighten the mood. "Way to make me even crazier than I already am. Seriously, don't sweat it, Aub. I just thought if there was anything you needed or wanted, any way I could help you, I would, you know?"

"Oh, I know," Aubrey said quietly, smiling now. "You're just about the best friend I ever had."

It was Emily's turn to stare out at the water. She felt tears welling in her eyes. Facing the lake, she could pretend that the warm wind coming off the water had brought them on. "I can wait," she said. "Only, when you say soon, what does that mean? Later today? Tomorrow, next week, next month?"

"Soon," Aubrey promised. "Really soon, I hope. Maybe next week. Cross your fingers for me."

Emily nodded. What else could she do?

Chapter Eleven

❁

A Sighting in the City

"Don't worry. She'll be here," Emily reassured LJ — and herself.

Emily had arrived at the Lasky twins' house — or the *ghastly* twins, as LJ sometimes called them — five minutes late. When she got there, she discovered that Aubrey hadn't shown up yet.

Carmen, LJ's sister, had, and was eager to get to the movie.

Emily was trying to convince LJ to leave, saying that she'd be fine, and that Aubrey would be there any minute to help.

The Terrible Two were holding on to LJ's

legs and looking up at Emily with their big, brown eyes.

If she'd believed everything LJ had said about them, Emily might have thought they were checking her out to see if they could take her down.

But that was crazy. The little guys were incredibly cute. They looked nothing like she'd expected from LJ's horror stories.

"Are you sure?" LJ asked.

"It's no problem," Emily assured her. "They're just babies. And Aubrey should be here soon."

Famous last words, Emily thought to herself an hour later.

For the umpteenth time, she had to scoop up another stuffed toy from the plushly carpeted family room floor, where the boys were wailing like emergency sirens while beating each other over their heads with teddy bears, alligators, bunny rabbits, and a large stuffed carrot.

The toys were soft, but the blows were hard. And when Emily picked up one bawling boy, the other one had a fit — a kicking, screaming, sippy-cup-tossing fit.

When she had a moment, which was almost never, Emily wondered and even worried about Aubrey. Where was she? Why hadn't she called?

Everett, the toddler she was holding, began to buck and kick in her arms, pummeling her shoulder with his little fists. His twin, Elliot, lifted his arms and shrieked to be picked up from the floor, too.

A pair of extra hands would have made a huge difference. And if Emily could get to her cell phone, which she'd stupidly left upstairs in her backpack, she would have tracked Aubrey down and found out exactly what had happened. This time, no vague excuse would be good enough.

"Breathe!" Emily ordered Elliot, who had thrown himself on his back and was gasping for air. She set Everett down to pick Elliot up, and pudgy little Everett took off like a shot.

There was no time to chase him. Emily had to get Elliot onto the sofa, where she'd be able to give him mouth-to-mouth resuscitation if he turned any bluer. She tried to lay him down, but he clung to her like Velcro and wouldn't let go.

Holding and bouncing Elliot a minute later (he was not only breathing again but bellowing in her ear) she walked from room to room, trying to find Everett. "Come on. Where are you? Everett, this is not a game! Everett Ghastly — I mean, Lasky! You come out right now!"

Just outside the guest bathroom, Emily thought she heard something. With her hip, she pushed open the bathroom door. There was Everett, standing in the toilet, giggling as he soaked himself and splashed water all over the newly installed, outrageously pricey (according to LJ), plush, white wall-to-wall carpeting.

"Everett, what are you doing?!" Emily hollered, horrified — although what he was doing was pretty clear. Then she cried, "Oh, no!" as Elliot, who was twisting in her arms, spit up the Cocoa Puffs he'd wolfed down ten minutes earlier — when she'd had to wrestle him for the box.

Several times during the afternoon, Emily thought of calling Aubrey. This had been Aubrey's idea in the first place!

But there was no time. None. For the next hour and a half, Emily ran herself ragged. She managed to keep herself and the twins alive — a fact she was extremely proud of — but she barely had time to breathe.

When LJ got back, she took one look at Emily and cracked up. "Have you seen yourself?" she said when Emily scowled at her. "I warned you.

Don't say I didn't." LJ looked around. "So did Aubrey run screaming from the house?"

Emily didn't want to lie to LJ. But she didn't want to tell the truth, either. "No one would blame her if she did," was all Emily could come up with.

On the way home, exhausted, Emily checked her messages. There were two from Aubrey, just saying, "Call me," and one from Jenna: "You'll never guess who we saw in the city! Get back to me ASAP."

Emily was surprised at how good she felt that Aubrey had called. At least she hadn't disappeared without trying to get in touch with Emily. The time of the first message was 1:00 P.M., shortly after Emily arrived at the twins' house. The second message was from 2:30, around the time Emily had been hauling Everett out of the toilet.

She dialed Aubrey's cell, and when she got her voice mail, she tried texting her.

Nothing.

And nothing to do except return Jenna's call. Jenna, Emily was certain, would ask about babysitting the twins and how she and Aubrey had coped.

Emily didn't need to make up stories about Aubrey, but she wasn't in the mood to hear a whole lot of told-you-sos, either. She decided to wait to call Jenna — no matter how hot her celeb sighting might have been — until she'd taken a shower and recovered a little from her nightmarish afternoon with the Lasky twins.

"What took you so long?" Jenna demanded, when Emily finally returned the call.

"I was in a wrestling match with two toddlers, and they won," Emily told her. "So who'd you see in the city?"

"First, you tell me — did Aubrey babysit with you today?"

"Why?" Emily asked, a sinking feeling in her gut.

"Because I think I saw her in New York."

Emily put a hand over her cell phone, so Jenna wouldn't hear her sigh.

"And that's not even the big news!" Jenna had never sounded so giddy. "Guess who she was with?"

"Her mother?" Emily answered without thinking. Jenna wouldn't have gotten excited over seeing Mrs. Captain Foster in the city.

Jenna made an impatient noise. "Yeah, right. Think, Emily, think!"

"Are you sure it was Aubrey?"

"Tall, thin, wearing a baseball cap, jeans, and

a San Antonio Spurs T-shirt — San Antonio, as in Texas."

"Sounds like her," Emily was forced to admit. "So who was she with?"

"Tony Shaw!" Jenna shrieked.

"No way!"

"Way, way, way!" Jenna chanted ecstatically.

"What did Aubrey say?"

"Um, I didn't get to talk to her," Jenna admitted sheepishly. "Tony was wearing a hat and these huge sunglasses, but everyone recognized him anyway, and he was mobbed. I couldn't get to them."

"But you're sure Aubrey was with him?"

"Well, it looked like Aubrey," Jenna backpedaled. "Only, well, I was too far away to tell for absolutely, positively sure. And her hair looked . . . blond."

"Blond?!"

"Maybe it was the way the light hit it," Jenna argued.

"Maybe it just wasn't Aubrey," Emily said.

But it was. Hours after she hung up with Jenna, and minutes after the highlight of Emily's day — Tyler called her! — Aubrey was on the line, apologizing and swearing to Emily that she absolutely couldn't help being AWOL.

"I wanted to call you the minute I found out I couldn't make it, but everything happened so fast. Then I called, but your phone must have been off, and then I kind of freaked out and was afraid you'd never speak to me again. But I want to tell you the truth now, Em —"

"Let's start with this," Emily interrupted, already feeling stupid for what she was about to ask. "Were you, by any chance — and don't laugh — were you with . . . Tony Shaw today?"

"Yes," Aubrey said, sounding more relieved than shocked. "And I know how you know."

"Jenna saw you in New York. At least she thinks she did."

"I spotted her, too," Aubrey said. "I wasn't absolutely sure she saw me —"

"Well, she wasn't absolutely sure she saw you, either," Emily said curtly.

"I'm glad she did, I guess," Aubrey said. "I've been wanting to tell you what's going on. And I will, Em, only you can't tell anyone else. Promise?"

Emily paused. "No," she said after a moment. Despite her burning curiosity, and feeling flattered that Aubrey wanted to share a secret with her alone, she couldn't do it. "Not," she told Aubrey, "if I have to promise not to tell LJ or Jenna. If that's what you need me to do, I can't. You probably think that's stupid —"

"No," Aubrey said. "That's loyal. It's what makes you such an awesome friend."

"Well, I may not be awesome, or even a friend, if you keep ditching me." The minute those words came out of her mouth, Emily wished she could take them back. They were true — but they were also harsh.

"Oh," Aubrey gasped. "Oh, Em, I'm so sorry."

The only positive thing that had happened to Emily all day was that Tyler had called. At least *he* wasn't going to ditch her. He was coming over after work the next day for their first rehearsal.

Emily was bursting with the news. She wanted to tell Aubrey about it. But the moment she'd heard Aubrey's voice on the phone, she realized how upset she was at her flaky friend.

Now Emily wondered what annoyed her more: Aubrey's no-show that afternoon, or the fact that, despite everything, Emily was still dying to tell her about Tyler's call?

"Do you have any idea what being alone with the twins was like?" she asked Aubrey instead. "No, I don't think you do. You can't. Even though the whole thing was *your idea* to begin with! Without you there, I had to be an acrobatic octopus, Aubrey! If anything had happened to the twins — a scratch, a bruise, anything! — I would never have forgiven myself. LJ wouldn't have forgiven me, either."

"Em, even though there's no excuse good enough, I really want to tell you what happened. At least as much as I can, and as much as you're willing to hear," Aubrey said, her voice thickening as if she were about to burst into tears. "I know you're mad at me. And you have every right to be." She sniffled. "I won't tell you anything you can't tell Jenna and LJ, all right? Something really important is happening in my life right now."

"Oh, right. And that something is Tony Shaw," Emily grumbled.

"Tony's a part of it," Aubrey admitted, shakily. "But not the way you think. It's not absolutely for sure yet. And even at the risk of jinxing it, I'd tell you in a minute, but not anyone else. The whole thing meant that I had to go to New York. I didn't know about it until the last minute. I tried to call you, twice, even though I knew you'd be really upset. I did try. And then I was someplace where I couldn't use my cell phone. I can't tell you what I was doing there."

"So that's it? That's all you have to say?"

Aubrey sounded miserable. "I don't want to tell you more than you want to know. And I'm afraid to say, 'Trust me.'"

"You should be," Emily said quietly.

Chapter Twelve

❀

The Start of Something

The day after her trauma with the twins, Emily decided not to go to the club. That way, she wouldn't have to get into it with Jenna or LJ about the babysitting fiasco. She could give herself a day to cool off about Aubrey. Most important, she wouldn't spend the afternoon watching Tyler and getting nervous about their rehearsal that night.

She told her friends, including Aubrey, that the twins had totally worn her out, and that she was taking a time-out to recover.

Which was not what she actually did.

To her mother's surprise, she spent the morning cleaning the family room, where she and Tyler would rehearse. When she'd finished vacuuming and dusting and putting away the old newspapers and magazines her dad left on the rug next to his favorite chair, she turned her attention to what she would wear.

Something casual but cute was as far as she got before she remembered she hadn't had breakfast — and it was already lunchtime. She made herself a peanut butter and jelly sandwich, took two bites, and realized her stomach was as jumpy as her mind.

Emily was upstairs a little later, standing in front of her closet, stumped, when her cell phone rang. She answered it, and her mouth fell open. No "Hello." No "Are you feeling better?" It was Jenna. "What are you going to wear?" she asked right away.

So Emily (in a pale pink T-shirt, the moss cargos Jenna had picked out for her at Old Navy, and a pair of ballet slippers) greeted Tyler at her front door at exactly six-thirty, when he'd said he would be there.

"Hey," he said.

"Hi," she responded, leaning back against the door frame.

"Um." He gave her a dazzling, heart-melting smile — which she returned with a happy grin of her own. Until he asked, "Can I come in?"

She'd been blocking his way. Instantly, Emily could feel her cheeks burn. "Oh! Sure, I mean, of course," she said, beet red and rolling her green eyes at her own blunder.

Tyler flushed, too, as Emily stepped back, making room for him to enter the house.

"This should be easy. I mean, we know all the words," she said, leading him into the family room.

"I guess. I mean, I thought it would be easy, too, but I'm a little rusty. And it's kind of boring to just stand side by side singing. We'll probably need to rehearse a lot before we have something good enough," Tyler said thoughtfully.

Emily's back was to him, so she could grin like crazy. *Oh, how sad. We'll have to rehearse — a lot!*

Tyler had brought the song sheet with him. He handed it to Emily when they reached the family room. "So, any ideas about how to pump up the act?" he asked.

"Well," Emily said shyly, "we could get costumes, maybe?"

"Yeah," Tyler said, tugging at his sun-bleached curls. "My hair's not exactly vintage sixties."

"Oh, but I like it," Emily blurted. *Did I really just say that?!*

Tyler shrugged, but traces of a shy smile spread across his lips. "So, I guess we can start out just singing, right?" he said, all business again.

"Sure." Emily wished she'd talked more about their act with Aubrey, who always had such good ideas. And who, she suddenly realized, she wasn't that mad at anymore.

She propped the sheet music up against some books on one of the shelves in the family room. Then, standing at least two feet away from each other, she and Tyler began to sing.

Tyler was right about needing to rehearse. Even with the words staring them in the face, they both managed to mess up enough times to get them laughing.

"Hey, Taylor," Tyler said, "didn't you practice at all before I got here?"

"Does it sound like I did?" Emily giggled. "It sure doesn't sound like *you* did."

"You got me," Tyler confessed, laughing.

They dove back into the music, but their laughter kept bubbling up as soon as they hit the spots where they'd made mistakes before.

"I think we're in trouble," Tyler said, grinning.

"It's not exactly a winning act," Emily agreed. "Even if we got all the words down —"

"Which doesn't look like a sure thing." Tyler laughed.

"Half the kids at the club already saw our duet at school. You're right, we've got to do something to make it more exciting."

"Okay. I'll try to think of something before our next rehearsal," Tyler said.

And I'll call Aubrey, Emily thought.

Chapter Thirteen

❀

Summer Fest

That next weekend, it was finally time for the Summer Fest concert. Thanks to Aubrey's family connections, they had five seats in the first row, center! Emily had never been to a concert in Madison Square Garden before, and she'd never, ever had *front row seats* for anything in her entire life!

They could actually reach out and touch the lip of the stage. Even Jenna, who usually tried to play it cool, couldn't hide her white-hot excitement. She was kneeling backward on her seat, trying to see if she recognized anyone in the audience. Emily could tell that she was dying to wave and show off her primo position. But the aisles were as busy as anthills, with people constantly coming and going. It was impossible to find a familiar face.

The concert was scheduled to start in a few minutes — the 20,000-seat arena was already packed, and piped-in music blared over the speaker system. The audience seemed to be a sea of girls — some younger than Emily and her friends, some older — wielding cameras and glow sticks. Many of them had parents in tow. LJ's mom seemed just as thrilled to be there as the girls did. It was the first time in a long time, Emily noted, that she'd seen Mrs. Suarez aglow.

LJ herself was over the moon. She poured over the Summer Fest program, reading choice bits aloud to her friends. The concert featured four acts — Ryan Moran, a singer from the TV comedy *Ryan's Crib*; hip-hop group L'il Bo and the Peeps; sisters Dana and DeDee, who currently had the number one single on the charts. The headliner was Joey Youngblood, an actor and singer who'd starred in this season's most popular TV movie, and whose new single was already the most-played song on the iPods of nearly every girl in the country.

Best of all, Aubrey was actually there! As in,

in her seat before the concert even started. As in, in the flesh, not leaving voice mails that she'd be late, not with her mom at some "emergency appointment." As in, reaching up to an inflated beach ball that bounced in the air, punching it over to a row of cute guys, and grinning.

"You're such a flirt," Jenna teased.

"Takes one to know one," Aubrey lobbed back cheerfully.

Aubrey was even dressed as they had planned (well, as Jenna had planned), in jeans, a lavender baby-doll top, and ballet slippers. It was Jenna's idea for all of them to push their hair back with silky golden headbands and wear yellow nail polish.

They looked like four best friends who'd known one another forever. Emily hadn't told Jenna or LJ that Aubrey had ditched out on the babysitting gig, and now she knew why. The foursome were tight, and that felt right. Emily didn't want to do anything that might change that. She could only hope the feeling would last.

Suddenly, the piped-in music came to a jarring stop and the house lights dimmed, throwing the arena into darkness. The show was about to start.

Squeals of anticipation rose up from the audience. The aisle ants scurried to their seats.

Colorful neon strobe lights flashed from the stage, and a live band kicked in. A giant screen flashed the name RYAN in lightbulbs, lighting up the back of the stage. The entire place exploded in screams.

Guitar slung over his shoulder, Ryan Moran rushed from the wings to claim center stage and launched into his first song. A wave of fans rushed down the aisles, snapping pictures and taking videos with their cell phones and digital cameras. Not Emily and her friends. They were way too mesmerized to move. Ryan was so close, they were nose to nose with the tips of his shiny black hipster shoes.

Jenna, who'd never admitted to being a Ryan fan, was mesmerized; her mouth hung half-open, her eyes were big as disks. She was almost too enthralled to critique the young star.

Almost.

She leaned over to Emily and hollered, "Can you see that? He's wearing makeup! His face is practically orange — and look at that thick guyliner. Eww! Maybe someone should clue him in."

After a few numbers under the bright stage lights, Ryan's makeup started to melt. A bead of black-tinged sweat carved a tiny path down one of his cheeks.

Unfortunately for Ryan, the entire show was simulcast on huge monitors around the concert hall. That way, everyone in the audience (even in the nosebleed section) could feel up close and personal with the singer. Judging by their squealing reactions, they thought his makeup meltdown was cute!

LJ was staring up at the stage, beaming. Her mom, who didn't even know any of Ryan's songs, did them all one better. Mrs. Suarez was on her feet, waving her hands and dancing to the beat. Impulsively, Emily leaned over and hugged Aubrey, who responded with a knowing grin.

Ryan's fans loved his songs, if not his personality. The star barely acknowledged the audience at all, only pausing between numbers to announce their titles. Emily hoped, for LJ's sake, that Joey Youngblood was fan-friendlier than that.

Next up was L'il Bo and the Peeps, an awesome hip-hop act that had everyone in the concert hall up on their feet, trying to mimic the crazy onstage moves. The boys in the group popped and locked, doing splits and break-dancing as they traded rap riffs and melodic choruses. By the end of their twenty-minute set, everyone — performers and audience members alike — was drenched in sweat.

After a short break, when the girls cooled off and grabbed refreshments — cold drinks and long, twisty pretzels — it was time for sister act Dana and DeDee to take the stage. And it was time for Jenna to, once again, dial up her inner Nina Garcia, the hard-to-please fashion critic from *Project Runway*.

Over the screams and wild applause that greeted the rocker chicks, Jenna bellowed, "Don't they know that no one does pounds of makeup and fake tans anymore?"

Jenna wasn't far off. Both Dana and DeDee, who were sixteen and eighteen years old, were buried under layers of glitter-dusted makeup that made them glow in the dark, blue sparkles on their eyelids, and thick false lashes. "Hair extensions are so 2006," Jenna sniffed of their platinum blond tresses. Emily couldn't help giggling at her friend.

The duo had a slew of hit songs, and the audience sang along loudly. Every once in a while, either Dana or DeDee — Emily didn't know which was which — stopped singing, pointed her microphone toward the audience, and let the crowd take over.

When their set was over, the stage went pitch-black. It was time for the main event. Slowly, low lights began to rise. A band — guitarist, keyboard player, and drummer, visible only as black silhouettes — posed with their instruments at the back of the stage. Suddenly, multicolored spotlights began to dance above them. By the time the stage lights came up, a blindingly bright spotlight had fallen on one shaggy-haired, sunglasses-wearing, guitar-slinging rock star. At the same moment a voice — his voice — blasted from the speakers: "What's up, New York?!"

The cheers were deafening. Emily could feel the noise vibrations coming up through the floor and into her body, even though the band hadn't played a single note yet.

"I'm Joey Youngblood!" the figure shouted, whipping off his sunglasses and whipping the already hyped audience into a frenzy. "Are you ready to rock?" Joey didn't wait for an answer before he launched into "Waves," one of his hit singles.

The audience leaped out of their seats, dancing and singing along with Joey. Many rushed the aisles, cameras over their heads, arms outstretched to try and reach their idol. But four girls and one mom in the front row didn't need to capture Joey digitally. They were close enough to touch him.

Close enough to see the studs running down one leg of his jeans; close enough to see his white button-down shirt billow behind him like a cape when he dashed from one end of the stage to the other; close enough to be dazzled by the rhinestone treble clef in the center of his black T-shirt; close enough to note that his sneakers had a checkerboard pattern on them.

At first, Emily and her friends were too transfixed to move at all. Then they found themselves singing, dancing, clapping, and cheering along.

During his second song, "Give Me a Dream," Joey got down on one knee and leaned as far over the stage as he dared, reaching out to brush fingertips with as many fans as possible. Emily, LJ, her mom, Jenna, and Aubrey could see his eyes sparkle, his shaggy hair fall across his forehead.

Emily couldn't help noticing that for once in her life, Jenna Lutz was tongue-tied. There was nothing to mock about Joey Youngblood. He was all about his fans. In a 20,000-seat concert hall, he could make each and every girl feel like he was singing to her alone.

And then, suddenly, he was. Singing to one girl alone.

Joey signaled his band to stop playing, and

gazed out into the audience. "I have a confession to make: I don't have a girlfriend. I guess I just haven't met my dream girl yet." He paused. "Maybe she's here tonight."

Each sentence was punctuated by screams and squeals and shouts of "I'll be your girlfriend, Joey!" from the crowd.

"What do you think?" Joey shaded his eyes and scanned the audience. "Do you think my dream girl is here tonight?"

Amid the loudest screams of the night, Joey strode over to the edge of center stage. He was so close, Emily could see the droplets of sweat on his cheeks and chin. She could also see his eyes dart to — Aubrey!

Had he chosen her? Emily turned to see Aubrey's reaction, when something else caught her eye: Aubrey discreetly tossed her head in LJ's direction. With a nod and a knowing grin, Joey leaned over as far as he could and reached out . . . to LJ!

Shocked, LJ reached up to touch his hand. Instead of brushing fingertips, Joey grasped LJ's wrist and said into the mike, "How about you, girl? I don't think we've met. But we can fix that now."

LJ's jaw dropped. Her eyes went wider than Emily had ever seen them.

The band started playing "Anything's Possible," Joey's biggest hit. As he started to sing softly, he motioned for LJ to let him help her up onto the stage.

"Me?" she mouthed, pointing at herself with her free hand and shaking her head in disbelief.

Jenna and Aubrey shouted, "Go! Go!" but LJ panicked.

In a flash, LJ's mom slid an arm around her shoulders, hauled her out of her seat, and helped Joey pull her up on stage.

The shrieking was now eardrum-splitting. Every single girl at the concert was wishing she'd been the one in the front row, the chosen one.

Joey immediately wrapped his arm around LJ. Emily heard him whisper in her ear, "What's your name? Do you know this song? Don't be nervous, just follow me."

LJ croaked her name — then froze.

Joey smiled. "Pretend the audience isn't there. Just watch me."

As the music ramped up, that's just what LJ did.

She looked amazing! Her glossy black curls were swept up in her yellow headband, which matched the sparkling ballet slippers on her feet.

Joey began to sing, then put the mike in front

of LJ. There was nothing she could do but sing along with him. Like millions of his fans, she knew the words to all of his songs. This one, his biggest hit, she knew perfectly.

Joey looked proud of LJ, with his eyes focused on hers. Slowly, LJ got into the performance, smiling, singing, dancing, and having the time of her life.

Mrs. Suarez and Aubrey both started taking as many pictures as possible. So, it seemed, did every other person in the arena. Cell phones were lifted into the air to capture the sight and sound of Joey singing with the lucky mystery girl who'd sat in the front row.

Beaming, Aubrey pointed up to the big screen. "Look, there's LJ, fifteen feet high!" she cried.

Jenna screamed as LJ and Joey appeared, larger than life. "Look, look! Everyone's gonna see her!" Jenna squealed. "That's my best friend!"

Emily felt like her face would crack from smiling so much. LJ wasn't going to need any photos. She'd remember this forever.

Chapter Fourteen

❁

Star Power

LJ and her friends became stars overnight.

The *Franklin Lakes Gazette,* the local paper, had printed a shot of LJ and Joey singing together on the front page of the entertainment section. A clip was making the rounds on a couple of popular Web sites, too.

But the sweetest moment came the day after the concert, at the swim club. Skyler pushed through the group of excited kids surrounding LJ, Jenna, and Emily, and shrieked, "Oh my gosh, LJ, I couldn't believe it. I saw you on YouTube! You were singing with Joey Youngblood!"

"We were all sitting in the front row," Jenna remarked casually, as if she were *so* bored with having to explain the obvious over and over. "Naturally, Joey chose LJ. She looked amazing. I did her hair."

"Aubrey got us the tickets," Emily said, giving credit where it was due. "She's the one who snagged the best seats in the house for us."

"Aubrey? Where is she?" Skyler asked.

LJ pointed toward the water. Aubrey was doing laps across the pool, under the protective gaze of Jason Weiss, super-attentive junior lifeguard.

"That's not Jason, is it?" Skyler's golden tan turned a sickly, fish-belly white.

"Gee, let's see," Jenna said. "Tall, tan, glossy black hair. I think so."

"Oh, no. I hope Sara doesn't see him." Skyler sounded freaked out.

"Oh, no," Jenna echoed sarcastically. "She's watching him right now. And she doesn't look happy."

Suddenly, Blake appeared. Ignoring Emily, LJ, and Jenna, she grabbed Skyler's arm. "Sara wants to see you. Right now," she hissed. "You're supposed to bring Jason with you. He's going to show us the hip-hop moves."

"Hip-hop?" Jenna was on it in a flash.

"For the talent show," Skyler explained, without thinking.

"Skyler!" Blake rolled her eyes dramatically. "That was great. Just tell them all about our act. Sara will love that."

Skyler's color came flooding back, finally stopping at scarlet. "No one told me not to tell," she complained as Blake led her away.

No one but Jenna seemed to have cared about Skyler's slipup. "We can *so* win!" she announced once their adoring crowd drifted away. "The Ice Queens are going to do a hip-hop thing — yawn!" she joked.

"Ugh," LJ grunted in agreement.

"They can hip. They can hop. But they're so gonna flop!" Jenna chanted, delighted by her unexpected burst of poetry. "We'll totally destroy them. We're going to have amazing moves of our own. Aubrey's got them all worked out. And we're scouting costumes tomorrow at this place she knows, where we can get wigs and everything."

"I'm going, too," Emily reminded Jenna, turning toward the pool. Tyler was in the lifeguard chair now. He saw her and waved. She smiled and waved back at him, surprised at how natural it had begun to feel. But someone had forgotten to notify her face, which was suddenly on fire.

The evening after the Lasky twins nightmare, Emily and Tyler had realized that their duet wouldn't blow anyone away without some major work. By their second rehearsal, at Tyler's house, they could sing "Summer Nights" without cracking up. They had the lyrics and harmonies down — and Aubrey, Emily's secret weapon, had a plan for rehearsal number three. She was thinking about putting together a little backup group for them. The idea had sounded like fun to Emily, and Aubrey was convinced that it would be a snap to pull it off.

It struck Emily again how easily Aubrey had become the creative center of their group. She really knew how to have fun. Her ability to come up with cool ideas *almost* canceled out her unexplained, and sometimes seriously irritating, disappearances.

Aubrey came to join them now, drying her hair on one of her faded beach towels. "Hey, what happened to your fans?" she teased LJ.

"I could ask you the same thing," LJ said, jerking her head toward Jason, who was off duty now and on his way to the Snack Shack.

"Well, he's no Tony Shaw," Jenna joked, making fun of what she now thought was her mistake about seeing the actor with Aubrey in the city. Emily and Aubrey exchanged glances. Then Aubrey forced a bright, white smile Jenna's way. "No, but he's almost as cute!"

"Wednesday night. My house or yours?" Tyler asked Emily a little while later.

They were at the Snack Shack with Aubrey. Tyler was on his break, sipping water from the bottle he'd just pulled out of the cooler. Reef had joined them — and, seeing his friend at Aubrey's side, Jason had decided that he was thirsty, too.

"How about my place?" Aubrey suggested. "'Summer Nights' is in the karaoke songbook. And I've got some big ideas for your act."

"Sounds good," Tyler said.

"Yeah," Jason broke in. "What time?"

"I can definitely make it," Reef said, purposely ignoring Jason.

Emily laughed.

"This is for the talent show, guys," Tyler told them. "We're doing a duet, as in two people."

Aubrey ducked her head, looking down at her bare feet as if she were deciding on a new nail

135

polish color. "Um, I invited them," she said softly. "We were going to work out some moves —"

"I'm doing backup," Reef explained.

"Sorry, sucker," Jason said. "I'm doing the backup moves. Right, Aubrey?"

"This is so embarrassing," Aubrey muttered, looking helplessly at Emily.

Emily had just taken a big slurp from her plastic bottle. "Oh, no! I forgot," she gasped, sending water down the wrong pipe.

"Forgot what?" Tyler asked, but Emily was coughing, her eyes tearing up. She was afraid that water might blow out of her nose at any minute. *That would be attractive*, she thought, desperately trying to clear her throat.

"I was just thinking," Aubrey said to Tyler, "that you might want to do a little more with 'Summer Nights' than just stand still and sing it. I had some ideas for dance moves and a kind of backup group —"

"Cool," Tyler said, pounding Emily's back.

She finally stopped coughing and wiped her watery eyes. "Honest, Tyler, I meant to tell you about it," she said, her voice still raspy. "I mean, I meant to ask you. I didn't know we'd practice at Aubrey's, but I knew she wanted to try out some ideas and moves with a backup group."

"It's okay with me," Tyler said with his lopsided grin. "But why'd you pick these clowns?" He jokingly rolled his eyes at Reef and Jason.

Aubrey laughed. "I invited Keisha and Alyson, too. I think your song is perfect, but I just thought we could make it more talent show-ish."

"Is that even a word?" Uninvited, Blake had edged into the conversation. Emily stiffened automatically. "Jason," Blake said, "Sara's totally annoyed. You were supposed to meet us on the beach earlier, remember?"

"Oh, um . . ." Jason was on the spot. "I decided to work with another group. I mean, my hip-hop moves aren't that outstanding. I'm sure you guys can find someone better —"

Blake sighed. "I really don't think Sara's interest is all about the talent *show-ish*," she said sarcastically. Then she added, looking nervously over her shoulder, "Do *not* tell her I said that."

How come even when she's pleading, Blake makes it sound like an order? Emily mused.

"Excuse us, Blake." Aubrey matched Blake's frosty tone perfectly. "We're a little busy." She turned to Jason. "Are you with us?"

"Totally," he declared, grinning widely at her.

"You've been sarcastic, demanding, and mean," Aubrey said, turning back to Blake and smiling. "I'd say your work here is done."

"You'll be sorry," the Ice Queen said to Jason. Then she turned with a huff and clicked away on the sharp little heels of her metallic gold sandals.

Later that afternoon, Emily and Aubrey rode their bikes home together. In front of Emily's house, Aubrey hopped off her seat and stood straddling the purple bike. "You're such an awesome friend," she said abruptly. "Last year was a really rough time for me —"

"How come?" Emily asked, thinking that Aubrey might finally be ready to talk. "What happened?"

Aubrey turned her head toward the big maple tree at the curb. Its roots had begun to buckle the sidewalk. She inhaled deeply, then sighed, like someone about to take the plunge off a high diving board.

"Last year, I told two girls in my class, who I thought were my friends, that something was going to happen. They blabbed about it at school. Then, when it didn't happen, everyone was really mean to me," she said. "Some kids called me a liar. Some teased me. Some stopped speaking to me for the rest of the year. I was the laughingstock of the school. I might as well have had a bull's-eye painted on my back."

"That's terrible," Emily said. She felt awful for Aubrey. "I bet you're glad you're out of there."

"You can't imagine how glad," Aubrey told her, "or how good it felt when you rescued me from the Ice Queens that first day, and introduced me to Jenna and LJ."

"Believe me," Emily assured her, "I know how you feel."

On Wednesday, Keisha, Alyson, Jason, and Reef were already at Aubrey's when Emily arrived. The music to "Summer Nights" trickled out as she opened the door to the basement. She could also hear Keisha and Alyson belting out the chorus: "Tell me more, tell me more!"

At the bottom of the steps, Emily couldn't help cracking up. Jason, Reef, Keisha, and Alyson were stepping side to side, to the beat of the music. The boys pretended to comb their hair with big, over-sized combs that Aubrey had dug up. They also chewed gum loudly, making as many popping noises as they could.

Keisha and Alyson snapped their fingers as they sang. They were both wearing kerchiefs tied sideways around their necks, and straight-leg jeans with the bottoms rolled up, fifties style. "Hey, girl!" Keisha stopped singing and called to Emily. "What do you think? Not bad, right?"

Before Emily could answer, Aubrey ran up and caught her in a bear hug. "They're awesome," she said, motioning to the quartet. "Wait 'til you see the whole routine. Where's Tyler?"

"He'll be here," Emily said. She knew she could depend on him — and even on Aubrey, lately. Winning the talent show wasn't everything, but their chances had just soared, thanks to Aubrey. If she and Tyler won, Emily knew that she wanted to give their free club membership to LJ. But she hadn't talked it over with Tyler yet, she realized as he entered the room.

He took one look at the gum-snapping, greasy-haired backup boys and cracked up.

"Dude." Jason tried to sound casual as he hid his comb behind his back.

Reef reddened and frowned at Tyler. "Hey, man, we're here to help you out."

"Because Aubrey asked them to," Keisha teased. "Seriously, Ty, how cool do we look?"

"You do, you do." Tyler wound down his laughter. "No, really, guys. You all look great."

Reef tossed his comb at Tyler. "I'm over this," he told Aubrey.

"Cut it out," Keisha ordered. "We're just getting started."

"Let's take a break," Aubrey suggested. "We'll grab a snack and let Tyler and Emily use the karaoke machine, okay?"

"A snack with just you, me, Keisha, and Alyson," Jason teased. "Excellent."

"Not a chance," Reef added quickly, determined not to be left out. "What have you got to eat?"

When she and Tyler were alone, Emily laughed self-consciously. "Aubrey thinks we should move around while we sing. She thought maybe we could act out the words in the song."

"Which words?" Tyler asked, straight-faced. "Like, 'Met a girl, cute as can be'?"

Emily felt the heat rise in her cheeks. "No, it's 'Met a *boy*,' and it's my line," she reminded him.

"Oh, right." There it was again, the lopsided grin. "I get to sing, 'Met a girl, *crazy for me*.' I forgot."

Could I be any redder? Emily thought, trying not to freak out. "Yeah, after a gazillion rehearsals, you forgot." This time Emily's laugh came out sounding embarrassingly high-pitched. She

141

hoped Tyler didn't notice. The CD was already in the karaoke machine. "Let's just sing it like we always do," she suggested, "until Aubrey comes back."

They flipped on the music and sang the song through once, standing side by side, barely moving.

The second time around, when Tyler got to the lyrics they'd joked about — "Met a girl, crazy for me" — he turned to Emily with the sweetest smile.

She couldn't meet his gaze, even though she wanted to. Instead, she automatically looked down at the basement carpet. Emily barely remembered her next line. Then, very softly, she sang, "Met a boy, cute as can be."

Tyler bopped her lightly on the head. "Sing it like you mean it, Taylor," he teased. "I mean, I'm cute, right?"

He was joking, laughing at himself, not at her, Emily realized. She wanted to say, *You are, Tyler, you're really cute*, but she didn't dare. Instead, she raised an eyebrow and said, "Oh, I wouldn't go that far."

They sang the song again, flawlessly. They were able to look at each other this time, and sway to the beat, and get through all the lyrics without

Emily turning brighter red (as if that were even possible).

After the third time through, they began to get punchy. They started fooling around and singing the song different ways, with strange voices and accents. First, Tyler sang part of the song as if he were a weak, wheezing, creaky old guy, then Emily acted like a bumbling fool who couldn't get any of the words right. Tyler sang, in a Frenchish–Germanish accent, "Zooma eve I meet une girrrl." Finally, Emily began in an operatic version, singing a screeching soprano with Tyler jumping in with a glass-cracking falsetto.

"You've got a really cool voice," Tyler said, when they'd tired of laughing and trying to one-up each other.

"You, too," Emily said, enthusiastically.

"I'm not as good as you," Tyler told her. "Never was, never will be. Too bad you're so funny," he teased.

"Funny ha-ha or funny weird?" Emily took the bait.

"Both," Tyler said.

"I am not!" It only took a second before Emily realized that he'd set her up. He was grinning again. "Oh, sorry. I meant to say you're *fun*." He pretended it was a mistake.

"That's better." Emily couldn't keep a straight face.

"You know, I used to watch you — you and LJ and Jenna. You guys were always laughing and joking around," Tyler said. "But you, especially. I always thought you'd be fun to hang out with."

"Um, you, too." Emily managed to hang on to her smile even as she kicked herself for not having a cool and witty comeback. "Maybe we should keep rehearsing."

Tyler groaned. "I take back everything nice I said about you."

"Everything?" Emily challenged, grinning. "You mean I'm not fun to hang with?"

"I think you are," Aubrey chimed in from the stairs. "Your backup group just limped out of here. Too much rehearsal for one day." With an evil grin, she rubbed her hands together. "Now it's your turn."

Chapter Fifteen

❀

Stuff and Nonsense

"So what should we call you?" Jenna asked.

Aubrey's mom replied that if she had it her way, they could call her General Foster. But since she was only a captain, Mrs. Foster would do.

LJ and Emily laughed. Jenna seemed mildly disappointed. Aubrey slid down in the passenger seat and groaned at her mom's joke.

They were in *Mrs.* Foster's hybrid van, on their way to the theatrical supply shop to pick out costumes for the talent show. The store was only a half hour from where three of them had lived their entire lives. But it was Aubrey, the new girl, who had even known it existed.

Aubrey had gone online and tracked down half a dozen little theaters within fifty miles of Franklin Lakes. Then she'd contacted them to find out where they rented their costumes. Smart!

Mrs. Foster pulled into a parking space in front of STUFF AND NONSENSE, THEATRICAL OUTFITTERS OF BERGEN COUNTY. The building was two stories high and almost a block long. Emily could only imagine how much stuff was inside!

Emily was the last one through the door. By the time she got inside, Aubrey's mom was already talking to a short woman with black, rhinestone-studded glasses. The first floor was sensory overload, and not at all what Emily had imagined. This wasn't the kind of place that sold cheesy Halloween costumes or holiday decorations. It looked like a huge warehouse of endless disguises. There were racks and racks of dresses and suits of every style, brass-buttoned palace-guard gear, hoodies, military and Shakespearean-looking jackets, royal robes, evening gowns, and furs.

There were glass showcases filled with handbags, gloves, and over-the-top jewelry — sparkling earrings, tiaras, necklaces, and pendants fit for a queen. And there was a huge section of wigs, which was where Emily's friends were gathered now. They laughed, squealed, tried on hairstyles from every era of history, from Marie Antoinette to the eighties. There was even a perfect Elvis wig, which Emily imagined Tyler wearing for their performance.

"Emily, look!" Aubrey called. "Want to go blond?" She was holding a long, platinum wig that looked weirdly familiar. "You, too, can be an Ice Queen," Aubrey announced, and Emily got it. The wig looked just like Sara Livingston's hair!

"Maybe they've got a head to go with it," LJ joked.

"Yeah, an empty one," Jenna said. "Then it would really be Sara."

Emily hurried over to join her friends. To Jenna's delight, LJ was modeling the blond wig. Although she'd done it as a joke, it actually looked awesome with her caramel complexion.

LJ took off the wig and handed it to Emily, who tried it on, tucking her dark hair up inside. She checked herself out in the oval mirror nearby. She didn't look bad as a blond, she decided. Not as cool as LJ had, but . . .

"Not." Jenna shook her head. "That totally fades you out," she declared. "You were born to be a brunette. Anyway, I'm the one who's sup-posed to be Penny, the blond girl from *Hairspray*."

Jenna pulled the blond wig from Emily's head

and replaced it with a dark Rapunzel-style hair-
piece; its tumbling tendrils, like thick black vines,
hung nearly to Emily's waist. It looked silly, until
Jenna pulled some locks forward and draped them
over Emily's shoulders. "You look like a glamor-
ous witch," she declared.

Aubrey pulled the wig off Emily and plopped it
onto Jenna's head. While Jenna posed in front of
the mirror, cackling and making claws with her
hands, LJ said, "Let's check out the upstairs." She,
Emily, and Aubrey headed for the steep steps and
the sign that said PROPS.

"Props" could also have described the whole
store, as far as Emily was concerned. It was amazing. Aubrey had done it again!

The top floor looked like the jam-packed attic
of someone who had kept everything they'd
gotten since birth — if they'd been born when
dinosaurs roamed the earth. There were spooky
monster heads, giant puppets, and do-it-yourself
faces: noses of every size and shape, bushy eyebrows, beards, big ears. There were grandfather
clocks, thrones, delicate gold-painted chairs,
benches of every description, bedside tables,
chandeliers, and old lamps.

Aubrey tapped Emily's shoulder. Emily
shrieked. She was facing a hundred-year-old,

wrinkled and slimy monster head. A pair of amused gray-green eyes were visible behind the mask. LJ jumped in, waving a pair of gigantic, frog-green Frankenstein hands in Emily's face.

Jenna appeared upstairs just then, in a blond wig with stiff, U-shaped pigtails. But she freaked out when Aubrey turned toward her! Startled, Aubrey screamed, too. LJ doubled over with laughter, pounding her huge green hands on her knees.

"Girls!" It sounded like the rhinestone lady was at the bottom of the stairs.

The four friends clammed up instantly.

"Girls, come down here, please! I know exactly what you want, and it's down here."

Relieved that they hadn't been thrown out of the store for acting so silly, they barreled down the stairs.

"I'm Ruby, by the way," the woman said. She was holding a black, exaggeratedly stiff, bouffant wig — exactly like the ones from *Hairspray*!

Mrs. Foster smiled. "Isn't it perfect?"

It was! LJ tried it on. Even though it was the same color as her natural hair, the style completely changed her look. *She could be her grandmother — or mine,* Emily thought, remembering old family photographs.

Aubrey called, "Over here, LJ. Wait till you see this!" Emily and Jenna raced LJ to the spot where Aubrey was twirling around, holding a black-and-white checked dress — just like the one LJ's character wore in *Hairspray*!

"Oh, that is totally Tracy!" Jenna declared.

"It's perfect," Emily agreed, as LJ pulled it on over her clothes.

Mrs. Foster joined them, carrying black patent leather mary janes (which looked a lot like Tracy's dancing shoes) and a pair of short white ankle socks.

LJ kicked off her flip-flops, put a hand on Aubrey's shoulder, and lifted one foot at a time so that Emily could put the socks on her feet. The shoes were a few sizes too big, but LJ slipped them on, anyway. And there she was, Tracy Turnblad from *Hairspray*!

In less than an hour, all four girls were outfitted for the talent show. Emily had opted for her own hair instead of a wig; Aubrey promised she'd set and style it for *Grease*. She picked out a poodle skirt and blouse, a black leather motorcycle jacket for Tyler, black leather jackets for Jason and Reef, and pink and gray jackets for Keisha and Alyson. They'd all agreed: no Elvis wig.

The only bad part was that they had to leave

their outfits at the store. They were renting them for one day only — the day of the show. Mrs. Foster said she'd put the charges on her credit card.

While Mrs. Foster went to the register, the girls returned to the jewelry counter, where they were still hypnotized by the glitzy rings, bracelets, and necklaces. Emily glanced over at Mrs. Foster. When Ruby looked at the card that Aubrey's mom handed her, she shook her head. Mrs. Foster called Aubrey over, and Aubrey immediately dug another card out of her backpack. When Mrs. Foster presented both cards to Ruby, the rental went through. Before they left the store, Emily saw Mrs. Foster return one of the cards to Aubrey.

Emily was the last one to be dropped off at home. Sitting behind Aubrey, she got up the nerve to ask, "Was everything OK with the rental?"

"Oh, Stuff and Nonsense only rents to the trade," Mrs. Foster called over her shoulder from the driver's seat. "They just needed proof that —"

"Mom!" Aubrey shrank down in her seat.

"Um, it's okay," Emily said awkwardly. "I just . . . wondered, that's all." Funny how she could feel so close to Aubrey one minute, and so out of it the next.

Chapter Sixteen

❃

Got Talent?

Two weeks and four more rehearsals later, it was finally time for the talent show.

"Hey, what's up, everyone?" Andy Mariani, talent show DJ extraordinaire, did his best rock-star/TV-announcer imitation in the mike. Andy had volunteered to host for the evening and was clearly determined to have fun. He bounded onto the stage and welcomed the crowd to the annual end-of-summer Franklin Lakes Swim Club Talent Contest.

"We've got an awesome lineup — singers, dancers, musicians of all ages. But only one act can win our top prize! Who will it be? Oh, the suspense!" he hollered. "Everybody ready to roll?"

It was the Saturday evening before Labor Day. Emily's summer had whizzed by at whiplash speed. She wished it didn't have to end so soon. But if it did, she hoped it would end on a high note. She hoped that LJ would win the free membership, and that Aubrey would tell the whole truth about herself. Emily knew it was the only way the girl who'd set their fantastic summer in motion could really be a permanent part of their group.

As for Emily and Tyler, was it too much to hope that their duet would lead to a real connection? Like Sandy and Danny, their *Grease* characters, or Troy and Gabriella, whose singing brought them together in *High School Musical*. Emily had to laugh at herself. *Grease* and *High School Musical*? Those were fantasies. It didn't happen that way in real life. Not in her real life, anyway.

"A few notes before we start," Andy announced, trying to keep a straight face.

On cue, Pete stepped up beside him and strummed a few loud notes on his guitar.

Andy did his best to glare at Pete.

"You *said* a few notes," Pete said, trying not to crack up. "Notes? Get it?"

Emily laughed. There were a few giggles from the audience, but mostly groans. It was a long way to go for a cheesy joke.

All the performers who weren't about to go onstage sat in the audience. Emily, Jenna, LJ, and Aubrey, even Sara and her clique, were among them. They perched on folding chairs in a semicircle, facing the raised wooden platform at the back of the Snack Shack. The Shack served as a combination backstage area and dressing room. Tyler was back there now, Emily knew. He was running the sound system and was in charge of ushering each act onto the stage through the kitchen's back door.

"We'll start tonight," Andy was explaining, "with our youngest performers. Give it up for the Tadpoles!"

With that, the tots were trotted out. The audience clapped enthusiastically, while the parents of the smallest performers peered at the tiny screens of their video cameras. The littlest kids were decked out in ballerina tutus, cowboy hats and boots, superhero and princess costumes. The audience let out a collective "Aaaw!" as the kids fumbled their way through the theme song from *Little Einstein*. They reminded Emily of clumsy puppies. How could anyone not love them? Then

154

she thought about the Lasky twins. *Well, there* are *exceptions to every rule!*

Aubrey's eyes were glued to the stage. She gushed, "Could they be any cuter?"

Jenna's eyes, however, were glued on Aubrey. "You'll be here the whole time, right? You promised."

Aubrey shrugged and held up her palms. "Who can say?" She gestured at her cell phone.

"Turn it off!" Jenna hissed.

"It *is* off." Aubrey paused for maximum tease-effect. "It's on vibrate."

LJ giggled.

Jenna, realizing she was being played, went from anxious to red-faced. Aubrey was loving it! She bumped shoulders with Jenna, then twisted around in her chair. Mrs. Foster, a few rows behind them, waved. "*Her* cell phone's on," Aubrey told Jenna. "So we won't accidentally miss any of our *emergency* appointments."

Emily and LJ burst out laughing.

Jenna? Not so much. "Don't quit school," she snapped. "A career in comedy is not in your future."

Aubrey pressed her lips together, a mischievous sparkle in her eyes. "We'll just have to see about that."

Onstage, Andy was introducing the next group. Kids going into first and second grade, dressed in homemade costumes of Princess Fiona, Donkey, and the big green ogre Shrek traipsed out onto the stage. They performed songs and dances from *Shrek*, including Emily's personal favorite, "Accidentally in Love." They butchered it. Emily cringed. But then she caught a glimpse of Tyler, peeking out the back door of the Snack Shack, and smiled.

The next group of performers were the kids going into third, fourth, and fifth grades. The junior-high-aged groups were next!

Emily's stomach did a somersault. It wasn't just going on stage that made her nervous — it was singing with Tyler. *How horribly will I mess up?*

Up to this point, Emily had managed to quiet her butterflies, but these middle-grade kids were good. One brave girl brought out her guitar and sang a Hannah Montana song. Then two girls did a dance and gymnastics routine.

The cutest fifth grader, Coles, a dimpled, platinum-blond-teen-idol-waiting-to-happen, turned out to be an excellent singer. When he tossed his baseball cap into the audience at the end of his performance, girls screamed!

Emily and Aubrey applauded loudly. LJ whistled with two fingers in her mouth. Emily saw Jenna quickly scan the judges. They were parents and teachers whose own children were not competing, and they looked like they loved what they were seeing.

Jenna gulped. "Could we actually lose to the tweeners? I mean, they're, like . . . good!"

"Thanks," Emily said sarcastically. "Do I look like I'm short on anxiety right now?"

Next, a keyboard was rolled onto the stage, and Andy announced, "Put your hands together for Yelena Robinov, who will play a song she composed herself."

That was the cue for Emily, her friends, and all the junior high performers to head backstage and get ready. It was their turn to strut their stuff — or fall totally flat.

Their clothes, wigs, shoes, and accessories were in camo-colored duffel bags supplied by Mrs. Foster. She'd lined them up in the curtained-off girls' changing area.

Jenna was not happy with the order of performances. It was supposed to be random. As she put sixties-style blue eye shadow on Aubrey, she huffed, "Why do *they* get to go last?"

Sara, Blake, and Skyler, doing their hip-hop routine to a Beyoncé hit, were listed as the final act. "Everyone knows that whoever is on last has a chance to make the best impression on the judges," Jenna grumbled, shimmying into the jumper she was going to wear on stage. "If they win, I'm so protesting."

"Relax, Jenna," Aubrey said. This time, she was serious. "We're better than they are. Trust me."

"How do you know?" Jenna challenged, crossing her freckled arms. "Have you seen their act?"

"I've seen ours," Aubrey responded calmly. "We rock."

Amazingly, Jenna did chill out. But not for long. The girls were about halfway dressed when Sara, Blake, and Skyler pushed the curtains apart and marched in.

"What are you doing here?" Jenna snapped.

"Waiting for our turn to get ready," Sara said coolly. "We're on after you. As you probably know."

"The courteous thing to do is to wait outside. As *you* probably know," Emily was surprised to hear herself retort.

"Too bad we're not here to be courteous. We're here to win." Sara smirked.

Blake was the first to notice their costumes. "Where'd you get this?" With two fingers, she picked up Jenna's blond wig.

Skyler jumped in. "Look, it's the checkerboard dress, just like in the movie! And the wigs — they're . . . they're like exact copies. What'd you do, steal the wardrobe from the movie?"

"The only thing we're gonna steal," Aubrey said softly, "is the show."

Sara must have heard her. She crossed her arms and tried to stare Aubrey down with her famous evil squint. "Bring it on."

"I say we ignore them," Jenna instructed. "Everyone else will."

As Sara and her sidekicks stalked away, Emily fumed. Where did the Ice Queens come off barging in on them like that?

That was the mood Tyler found her in, just before the two of them were about to go on stage. At the sight of him, Emily's fury dissolved. Tyler had worked hard to slick back his hair, and he looked great in his jeans, leather jacket, and black tee. Emily was tongue-tied.

Jenna was not.

"Tyler, you're a rock star! Every girl in the place is going to fall for you."

"Too bad," he said, pretending to slick back his already greased hair. " 'Cause tonight, I'm all about Sandy."

Sandy? That was her! Emily blushed and pretended to pick a loose thread off of her poodle skirt. How would she ever get through this song? She was too nervous!

Just then, LJ sidled up to her, whispering, "Remember when I was on stage with Joey Youngblood? I was so nervous. But once we got going, it just felt right. Like you and Tyler, Em."

At that moment, Emily knew there was nothing she wouldn't do for LJ tonight — including stomping Sara and her snotty sidekicks.

"And now!" Andy's voice boomed from the stage. "Give it up for Sandy and Danny from *Grease* — better known as our very own Emily and Tyler!"

Everything after that was a blur.

First, the backup singers, Keisha, Alyson, Jason, and Reef, dashed out. Their costumes and attitudes alone were enough to set off a round of applause and laughter from the crowd.

Then, Tyler grabbed Emily's hand and ran onstage. She trotted along, picking up on his confident vibe, getting into character. The audience clapped its approval when they appeared. Backstage, Pete started the karaoke machine.

The music blasted, and suddenly, it felt natural for Emily to slide into the routine they'd practiced. They became Sandy and Danny, trading lines about different versions of their summer romance while Jason and Reef combed their hair, and Keisha and Alyson urged, "Tell me more, tell me more."

This time, Emily wasn't nervous at all when she sang, "Met a boy, cute as can be." She knew exactly what she was supposed to do. Aubrey had choreographed their song perfectly!

At the end of the song, Emily and Tyler posed back to back, arms folded. The applause, loud and long-lasting, broke the spell for Emily. She morphed quickly from Sandy to Emily. She was back in Franklin Lakes, her heart beating fast, but her confidence soaring. Emily was pretty sure that the whistling and clapping was led by her proud parents in the third row. Her eyes found LJ's mom, and Jenna's family, and Aubrey's mom, too.

But Mrs. Foster wasn't clapping. She was on the phone.

Emily's stomach flopped. No way would she take Aubrey away right now — they were about to go on!

She wouldn't.

She couldn't!

She didn't.

As Emily and Tyler took their final bows and headed offstage, they high-fived the *Hairspray* girls, going the other way. The trio dashed onstage as Andy hollered, "From *Hairspray*, I give you three girls who can't stop the beat — Penny, Edna, and Tracy, or, as we know and love them — Jenna, Aubrey, and LJ!"

With the first note, the threesome took off, blowing the audience away with their costumes, choreography, makeup, and singing. They had memorized every verse of the upbeat song, and soon had the entire audience up on their feet, dancing and singing along! Emily thought, *If you didn't know this was an amateur production, you would have sworn you were in a Broadway theater!*

From the wings of the stage, she glanced at the judges. All of them were dancing and doing the hand motions along with Aubrey, Jenna, and LJ. Emily cheered, wriggling with excitement. Her friends were definitely going to win — it was practically in the bag!

Tyler hip-checked her, and the two of them started to sing along. So did Reef, Jason, and everyone else in the Snack Shack.

Except, of course, Sara, Blake, and Skyler.

Emily did catch a little toe-tapping from Skyler, and some barely visible lip-synching from Blake — until Sara glared at them.

Emily peered out into the audience to check on Mrs. Foster. She was no longer on the phone. Instead, she was beaming and giving Aubrey two thumbs-up. Aubrey reacted by doing an impromptu cartwheel across the stage!

A minute later, Aubrey headed off the stage as if it were all part of the act — which Emily knew it wasn't. Jenna and LJ didn't skip a beat. They continued the routine and kept the audience finger-snapping, singing, and dancing along with them.

But where was Aubrey?

"I totally cannot believe your friend," Jenna said to Emily, as she came off the stage after their number. "She pulled her disappearing act again. Right in the middle of our song!"

"It was at the end, not in the middle," Emily reminded Jenna. "And that cartwheel she did was amazing — when did you guys work that into the routine?"

"Uh, never," LJ said. But Emily could tell that she wasn't angry, just excited. They'd done exactly as they'd rehearsed, no slipups, and the swim club audience — along with the judges — had been completely into it.

The Ice Queens were up next. Emily almost felt sorry for Sara and her clique, having to follow the *Hairspray* trio!

Instead of the big finish Jenna had worried about, Sara, Blake, and Skyler's hip-hop routine — though it *was* really good — was anticlimactic. An afterthought. Because while Sara and her crew were on the final verse of their song, a strange thing happened.

The words they sang were "To the left, to the left," and suddenly, the entire audience turned . . . to the left!

A hiss of whispers that sounded like static began. Then they got louder. Emily flashed back to the night of the concert — that's what this noise sounded like.

A second later, she realized why.

He was — on the left.

He was standing in the left aisle, trying not to attract attention. A baseball cap, pulled low over his forehead, hid his famous shaggy hair and emerald green eyes. But no disguise could hide the fact that it was him.

Tony Shaw!

Chapter Seventeen

❀

A Shaw Thing

Even as her jaw dropped, Emily realized that there could only be one reason the movie star was there. Her name was Aubrey Foster.

And she was suddenly beside him! In front of a hundred pairs of wide, disbelieving eyes, he said something to her. Aubrey's arm shot up, her fist curled. "Yessss!" she cried.

Then Tony Shaw gave Aubrey a gigantic hug.

On the stage, Sara could be heard spewing her fury at Skyler, who had stopped singing and dancing and was staring at the celebrity, just like everyone else. "Tony!" she shrieked.

"You are so done!" Sara whispered savagely. "We are never talking to you again!"

The words, though whispered, were magnified by the microphones. As was Skyler's reply: "Like I care?"

Not that anyone but Emily, Jenna, and LJ was interested at that point, but the *Hairspray* group won the talent show hands down, and were called onstage to receive their prize. Jenna waltzed onto the stage, grabbed the mike, and called to Aubrey, "Get up here, girl. We're winners!"

Aubrey ran down the aisle toward them, with Tony Shaw in tow. To even louder cheering, he climbed onto the stage with her. "Hey, Franklin Lakes," he called. "You've got a real celebrity here." He held up Aubrey's arm.

"Aub, what's going on?" Suddenly, Sara Livingston was back on stage. She clasped Aubrey's free hand as if she were her best bud. "Hi, Tony," Sara said, blinking her heavily mascaraed eyelashes at the megastar.

Aubrey released herself from Sara's grip and turned her back on the girl. Not meanly. Not in the way Sara had deliberately turned her back on Aubrey that first day at the swim club. This time, it was just because she and Tony and her true best friends had formed a huddle. Inside of it, Emily asked, "Now can you tell us?"

"Try and stop me," Aubrey said. To the amazed audience, she turned and said, "Thank you so much for our win. We're very grateful." Then she hustled her buds backstage to the Snack Shack.

That was where Tony told them, "We're doing a TV series together. *Blond Ambition*. We've been working on it all summer."

Three sets of jaws dropped open. Before any of the girls could form an actual thought, Aubrey rushed to explain.

"The show is set in New York City. That's where I was most of the summer. We started shooting back in June. And the day I was supposed to babysit with you," she told Emily, "I'd just gotten word that I had to go to the city to meet with the big muckety-mucks, the producers and the sponsors —"

"Then it *was* you!" Jenna said, finally thawing from the silent, frozen state Tony's presence had put her in. "You were wearing a blond wig. I did see you in the city that day — both of you!"

"Blond Ambition," Emily said. "That explains the wig."

"What?" LJ was astonished. She glanced at

Emily. "Wait, you mean you watched the twins alone?"

Emily nodded, flashing back to what a horror show the cute little Laskys had turned out to be.

"I'm so sorry about that —" Aubrey started, but Jenna cut her off.

"We all saw *The Boy Who Could*," Jenna gushed to Tony. Once her mouth kicked into gear, it didn't stop. "You're definitely my favorite movie star —"

"But Aubrey," LJ said, back on the case. "Why wouldn't you want us to know about this? I mean, it's huge. You're going to be on TV! You're going to be a major celebrity. And we didn't even know you were an actress at all."

"I didn't want to tell anyone about it until everything was absolutely for sure, until we found out exactly when — or if — the series would air. So many things could have gone wrong —"

"But they didn't." Tony's grin, actual size, was every bit as warm as it was twenty feet tall on a movie screen. "I just found out that the series is absolutely, positively set to premiere this October. And Aubrey is also going to be in a bunch of print ads that kick off at the same time as the TV show. A toothpaste company is sponsoring our series —"

"The poster in your room!" Jenna hollered. "The one for Good-to-Glow toothpaste!"

Aubrey nodded and flashed a full, flawless smile. "Tony is doing ads, too —"

"Yeah, but it's Aubrey's ads that kick off the action. Aubrey Foster, coming to you on bus and magazine ads everywhere," Tony teased.

"I found out about everything yesterday, except the definite date the series would air," Aubrey went on. "I'm so sorry I couldn't tell you guys before. I was crazy superstitious. I auditioned for a movie last year and was told I got the part, but the financing fell through. The producers couldn't get the money together, so the movie was sidetracked —"

"But not before everyone at her school found out. Right, Aubrey?" Emily said to her beaming pal. "And naturally, some kids got jealous about it. When the movie didn't happen, they said she was lying, and word spread and, well, you can just imagine —"

"That's awful," LJ said.

"It was," Aubrey confessed.

"I'm so excited!" Jenna shrieked suddenly. "I can't wait to see you on TV!" She threw her arms around Aubrey. Then Emily and LJ piled on, shrieking and smothering Aubrey in a giant group hug.

Hours after the swim club triumph, after they'd gotten out of their costumes, and Tony had signed autographs until his hand ached, and LJ had collected the official swim club membership, and Tyler had asked Emily if she'd like to go out for pizza sometime, and Sara and Blake were seen trying to convince Skyler that they'd only been kidding about dropping her, Aubrey said she was too excited to relax.

"Me, too," Emily admitted. "I know, let's have a sleepover at my house."

"I second that idea," Jenna enthused.

"And I third it," LJ chimed in.

Aubrey's good news, the talent contest win, and getting up close and personal with Tony Shaw had left them wired. Alone, none of them would sleep tonight; together, none of them would care.

After a mass check-in with parents for permission, the unanimous answer was "Yes!"— except for Aubrey, whose mother was still yakking up a storm on her cell. *Probably*, Emily thought, *calling every relative and friend they ever had to spread the news.*

"It's okay. I'll be there," Aubrey said, pausing

for effect. "Unless, of course, my mom needs me to —"

"Don't even go there!" Jenna cried.

As promised, Aubrey showed up at Emily's later that night. In fact, she was a little early and the first to arrive. They ran upstairs together to Emily's room, where her desk and chair had been pushed into a corner to make room for sleeping bags on the floor.

Aubrey tossed her backpack and sleeping bag into a corner and flounced onto Emily's bed, where she flopped over backward. "I'm so psyched. And so relieved," she said. "No more secrets!"

"You know," Emily mused aloud, "I'm glad you didn't tell us everything right away. I'm glad we got to know you first. The *real* you."

"That's what I was hoping for," Aubrey said. "I keep remembering how you rushed over to rescue me from the Ice Queens. And how Jenna and LJ were so nice to me — until I started breaking appointments and not showing up when I said I would."

"Like at the twins' house." Emily tried to hide her smile.

"Yeah." Aubrey laughed. "I'm sorry. Honest, Em. And you covered for me. I couldn't believe it!"

"Neither could I," Emily joked.

Aubrey sat up suddenly. "Seriously, Emily," she said, "you've always stood up for me when I couldn't explain what was happening. You've always been there, Em, when I needed a friend. I've never ever met anyone like you."

"Excuse me?" Emily said, with a grin. "I think that's my line. I mean, I can definitely say the same thing about you. You're always there when someone needs something. Speaking of — did you set it up for Joey Youngblood to call LJ onto the stage to sing with him?"

Aubrey ducked her head, grinning. "I know it wasn't any of my business, but LJ was working so hard all summer, and I just thought she deserved a little fun."

"Oh, Aub," Emily said, "it was an awesome thing to do. LJ loved it so much. But how did you pull it off?"

"Joey Youngblood and I have the same agent," Aubrey confessed. "I met him at my agent's office a couple of times. He invited me to the show, and I asked if I could bring some friends. And I . . . well, I told him how much LJ liked his singing. And the rest is history." Aubrey shook her head and sighed. "You know, I was nervous, right up to today —"

"That the series would never air?" Emily asked.

"No, that things would change. That as soon as word got out, everyone would treat me like some kind of freak." Aubrey gave a little shrug and shook her head at her own silliness. "There was another reason I didn't want anyone to know," she said. "I was worried that once you, LJ, and Jenna knew the truth, you might treat me differently."

Emily giggled. "Of course we will. Now that you're going to be the most popular girl in junior high, I think we'll just drop you."

"Don't even joke about that," Aubrey said. "No, I finally got it. I knew I could totally count on you — just like I've been doing all summer — since you got to know me as *me*, not as some kind of crazy celebrity."

"Celebrity?" Suddenly Jenna and LJ appeared in the doorway. Jenna tossed her purple sleeping bag to the floor. "Did someone say there was a celebrity here?" She pretended to look around, hunting for one.

"Where?" LJ added, laughing. She laid a hand delicately on her chest. "You can't mean me? Little ol' me — the winner of the Franklin Lakes Swim

Club's first prize?" She ducked as Jenna lobbed a pillow at her.

Emily laughed and turned back to Aubrey. "I don't think you have anything to worry about."

Acknowledgments

Randi Reisfeld would like to thank Shannon Penney and the Scholastic Book Clubs for giving her the opportunity to write this book. She gives major props to her writing partner, H.B. Gilmour, who brought creativity, imagination, and brilliant writing "skillz" to this book.

About the Authors

Randi Reisfeld has been making waves as an author for ten years. Before that, she interviewed and wrote about celebrities for *16* magazine. Many of her current books are set in Hollywood and Malibu.

If you like reading books like that, look for her teen books *Starlet*, *Everyone Who's Anyone*, and *All Access*; or her popular middle grade series, T*Witches, online or at your favorite bookstore now.

Randi loves writing as much as *Making Waves*' Aubrey loves acting; and they both know that friendship is the most important thing of all.

H.B. Gilmour is the author of more than thirty novels and novelizations for adults and young readers. Among her works are several books based on the film and TV series, *Clueless*; *Godzilla*, which received a Nickelodeon Kids' Choice nomination; and, with writing partner Randi Reisfeld, the teen book T*Witches series. The first book in this bestselling saga of twin witches separated at birth was the basis for two made-for-TV Disney Channel movies. H.B. lives in New York's Hudson Valley with her husband, John, and their enormous and energetic lab, Harry.

check out

THE SISTER
SWITCH

By Jane B. Mason
& Sarah Hines Stephens

Another

Candy Apple book . . .

just for you.

Candy
Apple

CAITLIN

Thwack! My sister's foot connects with the ball. It's headed right toward me, but I don't even bother to look up from my book. First of all, I'm right at a really good part. Second, despite the fact that I'm sitting in a chair placed in the middle of the goal in our backyard, I am one hundred percent positive that the ball won't hit me. It never hits me — Andie's kicks are too good.

"Score," Andie shouts as the ball sails into the high right corner of the net. "That's fifty-two!"

"Yeah, but who's counting?" I tease. Now that I've finished the chapter I look up for a second, and Andie flashes me a smile.

"I am, of course." She grins and raises an eyebrow.

I know she wishes I would actually play goalie instead of just sitting here reading, but that's never going to happen. I almost never play soccer with Andie. Besides, this book is great. I really want to finish it before school starts, which means I only have until . . . tomorrow!

I dive into the next chapter while Andie flops down on her back in the grass with her ball. Her head is on the ground to my left and I can feel her gazing up at me with her green eyes — eyes that are exactly like mine. Actually, her whole face is exactly like mine, with maybe a few more freckles from all of the time in the sun on the playing field. The only other difference in our appearances is that she *always* wears her shoulder-length thick brown hair pulled back, and I *always* wear mine down. Other than that, we're identical, as in identical twins.

"Hey, Cait," Andie says, and waits.

"Hey, Andie," I say back, giving up on reading and closing my book around my finger to mark my place. I take a look at her face and know exactly what's on her mind. "You're thinking about school, huh?" I can read her thoughts as easily as my novel. It's a twin thing. And I might as well give up on reading for now, anyway, because between my sister giving me the silent "let's talk" look and my own excitement about starting school, I've read that last paragraph about five times. I'm still not sure exactly what it says.

Andie nods and tosses the soccer ball into the air over her stomach, catching it easily. "Can you believe that in less than twenty-four hours another glorious summer will be gone like the wind?"

I wrinkle my eyebrows and look down at her. Andie never uses similes like "gone like the wind." "Since when are you a poet?" I want to know.

"Didn't I tell you? I'm turning over a new leaf for junior high. I'm going to become . . ." she puts on her best serious expression and says, "scholarly."

I let out a whoop and shove her with my foot. "That'll be the day!" I laugh as I slide out of my chair and onto the grass next to her. "The same day I become a jock!"

It's pretty amazing, actually, how Andie and I can *look* exactly the same but *be* totally different. Andie is super-sporty and has an entire squad of friends. Mom says she has an "overdeveloped social life," and in the past it hasn't left her a lot of time for academics.

Me? I'm more into music than sports, and I love school. I always make honor roll and

Andie keeps predicting that I will be the class valedictorian someday. I tell her it will never happen because I'd have to give a speech at graduation, which I would never do. Talking in front of a crowd makes my knees wobble and my stomach head for the hills. But maybe I'll be able to figure something out before then. After all, graduation is pretty far away.

One thing Andie and I do have in common, besides our looks, is that we are both totally excited about starting at Woodland. Being in junior high means we've conquered elementary school and are moving onward and upward — new teachers, new students, new everything!